Shadow GAME

KAY MAREE

Contents

COLIN JOHN WILLIAMS
1947-2006

Dedication

Pop,
I can't begin to tell you how much you're missed.
There isn't a day that passes where I don't think about you, or talk
to my children about you.
You were many things in your life – a Boxer and a Racer, just to
name a couple.
But to me, you were, Pop. A man I looked up to, a man I admired.
This book is for you, Pop. I know you would have been proud of
me.
Love you always xx

Cover – Susan Horsnell
Editing – Susan Horsnell & Word Writer Pro

Social Links

Facebook:
https://www.facebook.com/kay.maree.334
Twitter:
https://twitter.com/MisKay85
Goodreads:
https://www.goodreads.com/book/show/34528910-angel-mine?ac=1&from_search=true
Goodreads Author Page:
https://www.goodreads.com/user/show/65394903-kay-maree

About the Author

I live in Newcastle, on the New South Wales coast of Australia with my husband and three beautiful children.

Between being a taxi for my children, and working full-time, I somehow find the time to write. It's something I love with a passion and with the encouragement of my very supportive husband, I have accomplished one of my dreams – releasing my first novel.

I hope you fall in love with my characters as much as I have.

I love reading and getting lost in a good book when I manage to snatch five minutes to myself.

Kay Maree

Chapter One

Leia

"Hello?" I hold the phone to my ear with a shoulder while I sit on the edge of my bed trying to pull on a pair of black jeans. Cursing myself for buying the tightest fucken jeans ever made, grrr.

"Leia"

"Oh, hi Ryan." I'm breathless, thanks to the wrestling match with my pants, and a little confused as to why he's ringing me. I glance at the clock on my nightstand wondering if I'm running late for our date.

"Leia, we need to talk."

Fuck, that doesn't sound good. I stop struggling with my jeans, reach up and grab my phone. I inhale and exhale slowly, wondering where this conversation is going. But, in all honesty, I knew it was coming.

"What's up?" I hope my voice sounds void of any, and all, emotion.

He chuckles nervously before he goes on, "how do you make those two words sound like a business discussion?" he mumbles lowly.

I sit up a little straighter when I hear his words. I don't think he meant for me to hear him, but I did, and it kind of hurt. He makes me sound so cold. He keeps speaking so I don't get a chance to say anything.

"I'm just going to cut to the chase, I don't think this thing we have going on is working."

I nod as he keeps speaking even though he can't see me. "I would really like to use that old saying of 'It's not you, it's me,' but I won't lie to you - it is definitely you. I didn t say that to hurt your feelings, and you're a nice girl, but I just don't see this going anywhere."

He hurriedly speaks the last words, and I wipe away the single tear which has slipped down my cheek, determined not to let him know his words hurt. I take another small breath in and out, slowly release it so my voice doesn't break when I speak. "Okay."

"Okay?" He sounds puzzled.

"Well, what would you like me to say? You have obviously made up your mind so, there is no point arguing with you." I note the edge to my voice.

"You must have known this was coming, Leia. You're so unresponsive and closed off. How the hell am I supposed to get to know you when you block me at every turn?"

"Well, I guess it's not your issue anymore, Ryan. You can..."

He cuts me off before I can finish the sentence. I feel anger slide up and down my spine wondering why the fuck I put up with this prick for the last four months.

"Look I'm sorry, okay. Fuck, I didn't ring to upset you I just thought..."

I cut him right back the fuck off. Fuck him, and fuck this conversation, or whatever the fuck it is.

"Are you done?"

Ryan pauses for a moment on hearing the sharp edge to my voice. "Yeah, I'm done."

He sighs with frustration, probably because I cut him off.

"Good." I don't let another word come out of his mouth, I click *end call* on my phone. I squeeze it in my hands wanting to throw it across the room, but I resist, knowing he is so not fucking worth it.

"Arrrgh." I throw myself back on the bed and look up to the ceiling watching the fan spin in circles while my mind replays his words. So, what if I'm a little closed off? I won't change who I am for anybody, especially a spineless, self-obsessed prick like him. I groan and kick off my jeans, no point putting them on if I'm not going anywhere.

I have two options now. I can crawl under the covers, stuff myself on ice cream and all the junk food I can get my hands on while I watch my all-time favorite movies - *Dirty Dancing, Cry Baby* and then finish off the movie marathon with *Grease*. Or, I can put some music on and dance around in my underwear. My ass might thank me if I choose option two, I snort at the thought.

Getting to my feet, I study myself in the floor length mirror in the corner of my room next to the built-in wardrobe. I run my fingers through my long thick black hair, putting it back into place after laying down. Pushing the black rimmed glasses back up on my nose brings attention to my hazel eyes. I scan my eyes down the rest of my pear-shaped body, dressed only in a black off the shoulder shirt and red lacy knickers. Rolling my eyes at myself, I groan, not giving two shits what I look like right now. Turning away from the mirror, I head from the bedroom into the living room.

My apartment is small, but since it's only me and my beautiful puppy, Elvis – yes, I named him after the one and only King of Rock 'n' Roll - this place is enough for us. The living and kitchen are open plan, and the place has an old school 50's style to it that I love. Thinking about *The King,* I know exactly what I need right now. I zero in on my ipod which is plugged into my stereo system. The system sits on the cabinet underneath my sixty-inch television which hangs on the wall. I flick through the playlist and find the perfect song to play. *This will do nicely,* I think to myself. Pressing play, and turning up the volume, I let the music flow through me as the lyrics of *Blue Suede Shoes* belts out. The music seems to soothe my soul and my body moves to the beat.

~*~

I'm not sure how long I was lost in my *Elvis* haze, but I haven't felt this free in a long time. I knew Ryan breaking up with me was coming, and I wasn't sad about it. I was more hurt by his words than anything else. Looking back, I should have ended things after our first date. I knew then he wouldn't be able to handle my kind of crazy, but I was sick of being alone and I guess I thought he could fill that empty space. Boy, was I wrong! He didn't fill any lonely spots inside me, instead, I had to cater to *his* ego. Constantly reassuring him he was the best thing in the fucking world, when at the end of the day, he wasn't all that good at anything besides annoying the shit out of me. I can't even think what attracted me to him to begin with.

I shake my head not wanting to think of him anymore and hear the first beats of *Jailhouse Rock* start to play. I shake my hips and start swaying and shimmering around my living room until I hear a chuckle behind me. I swing around to find my best friend, George leaning against the wall near my front door, his arms are crossed over his wide chest. I smile and head to the stereo to turn the music down.

"Hey ya snookums." I wink and on wiping my forehead, realize how sweaty I am. "Ewww." I flick my wet hand into mid-air.

Georgie starts laughing, a deep belly laugh, and I can't help but join in.

"Let me guess you and Ryan broke up?"

I narrow my eyes wondering how the hell he knows.

He shakes his head, and smiles at me before heading toward the kitchen. He pulls the water jug from the fridge, reaches above and takes two cups from the cupboard.

"How did you know I broke up with Ryan?" I take a seat at the breakfast bar.

He looks at me like I should know the answer, but when I raise my eyebrows he waves his hand toward my stereo and then toward me like it should be obvious. When I keep looking at him, he finally clues me in.

"You have music blaring, I'm amazed you aren't having heart palpitations with how loud it was and you're dancing around in your underwear." He chuckles. "I'm guessing you went with option two instead of junk food and movies."

My shoulders sag with the knowledge, I'm so transparent.

"Lee Lee, you forget how well I know you."

"Well shit," I grumble which starts him laughing again.

When he finally stops laughing, he clears his throat and asks the one question I knew was coming. "What happened?"

I shrug my shoulders and glance around the room, trying not to make eye contact.

"Leia?"

I groan and rub my face with both my hands and say the exact words Ryan said to me on the phone. "Ryan said this thing wasn't going anywhere, and it's not him, but it's me." I groan at repeating the words, it pisses me off. "Why are you here, anyway?" My tone is snappy, I'm taking my anger out on him. I feel like shit for snapping at him so I quickly apologize, "I'm sorry, I love that you're here, but I don't want to talk about another failed relationship." This is why we're best friends, he understands when I'm pissed and doesn't push the subject.

"I came over to walk, Elvis"

Oh, I'm such a bitch. I'd completely forgotten, I asked him to come over and walk Elvis for me while I was on my stupid date, I wasn't sure what time I would get home.

"I'm sorry," I mumble, lowering my head and peeking up at him above my glasses to give him my best puppy eyes.

Georgie bites his lip to stop from laughing and when he manages to compose himself, he speaks, "You owe me now, you know that don't you?"

I groan, I know exactly what he is getting at and I shake my head.

"You can't say no, this will teach you not to spit your sassy attitude my way."

"How the hell Michael puts up with you, I'll never know." I shake my head and laugh when he wiggles his eyebrows up and down.

"Oh, I have my ways of keeping him happy." We laugh harder.

Once I get my breath back from laughing so hard, I take the cool water Georgie offers me and gulp it down, not realising how thirsty I was. Placing the cup back on the bench I slide it over toward him. "Thanks, I needed that."

"You looked like you worked up quite a sweat baby girl."

I nod my head.

"Okay, you go and get ready, I'm gonna take Elvis for his walk, then we'll grab a bite to eat before we head out."

I gnaw on lip trying to come up with an excuse to get out of what he has planned and then it hits me. "I can't, I have to finish the program I'm working on for Mr. Samson." I give him my best, 'I'm sorry' eyes but it doesn't work.

"It's Friday, you have all weekend to finish it, so no excuses. Go get your ass ready before I get back, and no sweats, you're not bloody homeless."

I gasp, pretending I'm insulted by his words. He laughs and I try hard not to join him. That's when I notice him in blue jeans and a fitted black button up shirt with his brown hair gelled back and blue eyes sparkling with happiness. We have been friends for many years and have been through so much together, and it's so good to see him happy. For a long time, he never seemed to laugh and wasn't happy. Until, the love of his life, Michael, came into the picture.

"Stop staring at me and go and get ready."

I bounce to my feet and salute him. "Yes sir." As I head to my room, his laughter follows me.

~*~

Wrapping my towel tight around me, I head from the bathroom to my closet. I pass my jeans on the floor but kick them aside, not even bothering to try and put them back on again. Sliding my closet door open, I scan the many outfits I have and choose a black high waisted skirt and black singlet shirt. I lay them on the bed before grabbing a thin red belt and red cherry heels. I was going to go with a pair of jeans, but after the phone call earlier, I need a little pick me up and this outfit might just do the trick.

Dropping the towel, I slip into my clothes. Swinging from left to right in front of the mirror, I take notice of how this skirt makes my ass look huge. Well, bigger than normal, but, then again, my ass is huge. I shrug my shoulders, cross to the dressing table and apply the right amount of makeup so, I don't look like I live under a rock and have never seen sunlight a day in my life. Grabbing my brush, I run it through my hair before wrapping my favorite red bandana at the top of my head. To complete the look, I apply red lipstick which has the effect of making my lips look pouty and bee stung.

A whistle from the door draws my attention and I turn to see Georgie watching.

I raise a questioning eyebrow and wave my hand up and down my outfit, checking if it's okay.

"That's better," he smiles. "I seriously thought you would dress in sweats just to annoy me."

"I can always change, it's not too late." I smirk at the face he pulls.

"You would too wouldn't you, bitch"

I gasp, and throw my hand on my chest, at his words making him laugh.

"Okay, let's go before you start to annoy me." Georgie turns away from me.

"What do you mean start, I have to finish before I can start again." I watch as he heads out to the living room mumbling some shit I don't catch.

I laugh as I grab my clutch purse off the bed, and make my way toward the front door where Georgie is standing. "God, you drive me bloody crazy woman."

"But, you love my brand of crazy." I wink, and head out the door laughing.

Georgie nods his head, and mumbles he has no choice in the matter, which only makes me laugh harder.

Entering the Karaoke Bar on Beaumont Street, I glance around and note the small stage with coloured lights scattered above. There is a small platform off to the side where the DJ is positioned and wave to Michael who is currently setting up the speakers.

"I didn't expect to see you here tonight Lee Lee," Michael says as he moves toward us and wraps me in a big hug.

Before I can say a word, Georgie speaks for me, "I found her dancing around in her underwear, babe, I had to try and save her neighbours from *The King* so I thought I better bring her here." He chuckles as Michael wraps his arms around him and kisses his temple.

They are the cutest couple you have ever seen, and I feel my heart warm in the knowledge, Georgie has found an amazing man. I look around the bar allowing the vibe this place has consume me. I love coming here even though I whinge and moan about it, there's something freeing about getting up in front of strangers and belting out the lyrics to songs I love, and grew up with. I'm snapped back to the present when I hear Michael ask Georgie a question, I roll my eyes at the pair of them.

"Option two?"

Georgie laughs, and nods his head.

I roll my eyes again.

"I'm grabbing a beer, and leaving you two lovebirds to make fun of me in peace." I smile so they don't think I'm upset with them before crossing the room to the bar. I hear the two idiots laughing at my retreating back and give them a finger salute over my shoulder, making them laugh harder.

"Lee Lee so good to see you honey," Sharon says from behind the bar.

"You to Sharon, how have you been?" Sharon is in her early forties and she owns the bar with her husband, John. She is nice, and easy going, but if you piss her off, she'll have no problem throwing your ass out.

"Good sweetie, missed seeing your face around here."

"I know, I should come here more often, but I've been so busy with work, I haven't had a chance. I have one more program I need to fix for Mr. Samson, and then I can start working from home again. As much as I love getting out of bed, and having someplace to go during the day, nothing beats sitting around in my sweats."

Sharon nods her head, chuckling. "I bet honey, you singing tonight"

"Of course, she is." Georgie throws his arm over my shoulder and laughs when I narrow my eyes at him.

Sharon laughs as she places two schooners of ice cold beer on the bar towel in front of us.

"Thanks Sharon we're going to take these over to a table by the stage. Michael is about to start, and Lee Lee and me are up first."

I glance around the pub, and notice it's not very busy. Checking my watch, I see it's only 7pm. I didn't realise how early it was. Gathering my drink, I follow Georgie to the table, take a seat and a nice long mouthful of beer.

"Aaah, that tastes good," I say before taking another mouthful.

"Lee Lee, I don't want to be carrying your ass out of here tonight so, slow down," Georgie says. "We'll see." The first bars of 'I Will Survive by Gloria Gaynor' start to play, and Georgie grabs my arm, drags me up onto the stage, and hands me a microphone. We both start to belt out the words.

<h1 style="text-align:center">Chapter Two</h1>

Deacon

"You ready to go, Black?"

I nod my head in reply to my partner, Jim, as I grab my gun from the desk drawer and slot it into my holster at the side of my hip.

Jim has been my partner in the police force ever since I joined, when I was twenty years old and thought I knew everything. Jim quickly pulled me into line. I use to have a quick trigger when it came to criminals, but he has taught me how to control it. Even with ten years on me, he is my closest friend. He's tall, and like me, he stands around 6'3". At forty-one years old, he has dark hair with small streaks of gray scattered throughout.

"Did you call, Caroline?" I ask. Caroline is his wife of the last twenty something years, and as she tells the story, it was love at first sight and all that bullshit. She is one tough lady and is not one to be messed with according to Jim, she has a mean right hook.

"Yeah, I called her, do you think I could ever go home again if I didn't?"

I chuckle knowing he would have his balls in a vice if he didn't let her know we had an undercover op tonight.

Jim snorts. "You just wait, Deacon, your time is coming partner, I can't wait for the day a woman brings you to your knees." He chuckles when I shake my head at him.

"There is no way that's gonna happen. Enough of this romantic crap, let's get this shit done. Are you sure this guy is going to be at the bar tonight"

"Yeah, Pete said he likes to hang out there."

"We need to get this prick off the streets, Jim" He nods as we head to his car.

We've been after this prick for the past month, he likes to go to clubs and slip date rape drugs into girl's drinks. We only have this information because his so called girlfriend had a feeling he was cheating on her and followed him one night. She caught him and told us what he'd done. We thought we could get him when he next visited his girlfriend, but that option went out the window when she informed us, she'd thrown his ass out, and burned all his shit on the front lawn before coming to see us. So, we were in the position of having to track him down through other avenues.

We were lucky enough to arrest the guy, Pete, who sells him the drugs, and when we hauled his ass into the station, he couldn't wait to spill his guts in a deal for a lighter sentence. Jim and I were both pissed we had to stick to the deal, but we knew Pete would slip up again and we could send his ass away for a longer time then. So, that leads us to now pulling up to the curb in front of the Karaoke Bar in Hamilton.

"After we nail this fucker tonight, Caroline asked me to tell you to come over for dinner tomorrow night."

I accept, there is no point arguing because I know Caroline won't stop asking until I agree. Jim laughs, he knows it too. We test the earpieces and microphones are working before I leave the car and head to the bar ready to end this thing.

~*~

I give the bartender, a nice looking woman who informs me her name is Sharon, an order for a scotch, and while I wait, I swing around on the stool and survey the club. I take note of where the exits are, and check for anywhere else this fucker could slip out of without me noticing.

After thanking Sharon and taking my drink, I move to a high-top table alongside the wall, it gives me a perfect view of the stage and bar area. I take slow sips of my scotch as I listen to the music, and the people trying to sing. I cringe at a man singing, 'We Will Rock You' by 'Queen' knowing he is completely destroying a classic.

"That guy sounds like a cat on a hot tin roof," Jim chuckles in my ear.

"He's decimating a classic," I murmur under my breath.

The DJ announces the next song, 'Perfect' by 'Fairground Attraction' as my eyes again sweep the club.

"Holly fucken shit," I exclaim. The breath leaves my lungs, my mind zones out, and I forget about the jerk I'm supposed to be finding. It's as if I'm in a vacuum, and nobody and nothing else, exists at that precise time.

I forget about the earpiece in my ear and microphone attached to my chest under my shirt until I hear Jim. "What the fuck is wrong?" There is an anxious edge to his voice.

"I swear I just saw Betty Boop," I growl low, not wanting to take my eyes away from the vision on stage a couple of metres away from me. I suck in a deep breath when she brings the microphone up to her mouth and starts to sing. Chills crawl down my spine, and I feel my cock hardening in my jeans, straining against the zipper.

Her voice is drawing me into the depths of pure fucking ecstasy, I'm absolutely fucking captivated as I watch her hips sway to the beat of the music. I close my eyes to stop myself from exploding in my fucking pants, but it doesn't stop the myriad of feelings as her voice surrounds me. I imagine that husky voice whispering my name in the dark as I take her over the edge.

"Fuck," I growl before hearing Jim in my ear

"What, did you see Jessica fucking Rabbit this time?" he chuckles.

Fuck, why do I keep forgetting he's listening to everything. Shit, Deacon, get your head in the fucking game, we have an asshole to find and put away. I can't afford to be distracted right now. My pep talk doesn't work, my eyes fondle every delicious curve of her body and I lock eyes with hers. I fucking swear I'm in some kind of trance and she is singing only to me. I'm sure I see color rise to her cheeks, but it could be the lighting. I lick my suddenly dry lips, and my eyes zero in on her pouty red lip. I hold back a groan when her sweet pink tongue swipes across her bottom lip. "Fuck me standing," I growl low.

"No thanks buddy, you're not really my type."

I stay silent, embarrassed.

Jim starts laughing his ass off at my discomfort. I ignore him as I lower my head, and struggle to close my eyes. I steady myself by taking deep breaths in and out, attempting to gain control over these feelings she is evoking in me. I feel the loss of her eyes immediately, and for some reason, my stomach twists at the thought. Thank fuck the song is coming to end because I'm not sure how much more I can take. I have an unexplained need to pull her into my arms, and claim her as mine for all the world to see.

I plant my feet firmly on the ground, willing myself to relax. Remaining where I am, I silently count to ten before opening my eyes. I glance down at the glass of scotch in my hand, and realize how hard I'm gripping it, amazed I haven't smashed it to smithereens. Throwing the last of it back, I feel the liquid hit the back of my throat, and the familiar burn as it slides down my throat before settling in my stomach. I take another look around the club, trying to regain my bearings and get my head back in the game. I can't help but look for her, but she is now nowhere to be seen. Did I just dream her up?

"Remember only one drink," Jim orders, breaking into my thoughts.

I nod before realizing, he can't see me. "Yeah, partner I know," I eventually answer and shake my head at myself.

Fuck, what the hell just happened to me?

~*~

Leia

I step down off the stage on shaking legs, trying not to fall flat on my face. I look over toward Georgie, he's talking with Michael. I shake out my hands, I need a minute to calm myself. I hurry toward the ladies' room, squeezing through the throngs of people scattered all over the place. The place has become busy in the past two hours. Pushing through the door, I cross to the line of sinks, and rest my hands on a basin. Lowering my head, I take a few deep breaths in and out. Closing my eyes, I try to picture anything apart from green eyes which seemed to devour me whole.

I usually close my eyes when I sing, and let the music take over, but I couldn't break my eyes away from the man who was standing off to one side, leaning against a high-top table. I couldn't make him out completely as the house lights were lowered, and I had stage lights shining in my eyes, but I swear his eyes were green and they were staring directly into mine. I felt a strange connection stirring inside me, and without realizing it, I was singing directly to him. I lift my head and stare at myself in the mirror.

Get a grip Leia, why the hell would you sing to a complete stranger? I must be losing my damn mind. Turning the tap on, I run my hands under the cool water. I should have brought my clutch purse with me, so I could touch up my smudged lipstick. Grabbing pieces of hand towel, I dry off my hands then run a finger around the edge of my lips to clear the marks. Smacking them together, I hope to spread what little color is left, I guess it will have to do. After throwing the paper towel in the bin under the sink, I head back to the bar.

~*~

"Where did you go Lee Lee?" Georgie asks when I return to our table.

"The ladies room." I smile at him before asking, "are you up next." I nod my head toward the stage, and at the same time, I feel a hand grope my ass. Without thinking about it, I pivot and slap the smug bastard across the face.

"Don't you ever touch me again," I scream at the dickhead while he holds his face in his hand.

"Stupid bitch," he spits out.

I bring my hand back to hit him again, but before I get a chance to hit him, I'm pulled into Georgie's side and he loses his shit at him.

"You'll keep," the dipshit snarls.

I notice how dark and scary his eyes are, and try not to shrink back at the look on his face. I straighten and push my shoulders forward so he thinks his words don't mean shit to me.

He reaches for me again, but his arms are pulled back behind him and I gasp when I notice the man behind him. My eyes travel over a broad chest to a hard jaw, I notice a slight tick on the left side. Then, I'm staring into the same green eyes I was looking into from the stage. *They are green.* My mouth becomes dry, I lick my lips and watch as his eyes track the movement. I swear his eyes dilate before he scowls at the scumbag. I notice the music has stopped and everybody is watching what's happening.

"You have the right to remain silent, anything you say..."

I listen to his deep, mesmerizing voice as he speaks, and rub my arms as goosebumps break out. Fuck what that voice is doing to me.

"Are you okay baby girl?" Georgie wraps his arm around me, but I don't look at him.

I'm still staring at the handsome stranger in front of me as he pulls handcuffs from his back pocket, and snaps them into place. The sound of the lock clicking has heat crawling up my neck. For some reason, I picture him putting them on me and attaching them to the headboard of my bed.

I hear a throat clear and look up at the same time I see his eyes notice Georgie's arm around me. What looks like disappointment crosses his face, he mumbles something I don't hear clearly and stalks out of the club with the piece of crap in handcuffs.

~*~

"Lee Lee, damn girl, I swear you could have cut the sexual tension with a knife the way he was looking at you," Georgie exclaims.

I snap my eyes to him after staring at the exit for a bit too long.

"I don't know what you mean." I shrug, playing it off like it was nothing. Who the fuck am I kidding, it was far from nothing, but what am I supposed to do? Yell out to him, chase him through the club, and tell him I felt a connection between us? Yeah, like that shit ain't crazy, I'm nuts but that is a little crazy even for me. *Hey, did you know you looked into my eyes and I felt a connection between us, please don't leave me.* I snort at the different scenarios running through my head.

"What you snorting about?" Georgie asks as he sits.

I gaze at him, debating whether or not to tell him, and decide it might be easier to forget about it. "Nothing, but I think it's time for another drink." I grab my purse and head toward the bar before he has a chance to say another word on the matter, I need a minute to get my brain functioning normally again.

Chapter Three

Leia

A banging sound at the front door rattles my head and I groan, burying my face in my pillow in an attempt to ignore it. Hopefully it will go away, but, no such luck, the pounding seems to get louder. Who the fuck would be banging on my door this early in the morning? It can't be Georgie, he has his own key and would let himself in.

Groaning again, I roll to my back and crack one eye open. Thank God, I remembered to close the curtains before I dropped into bed last night, or maybe Georgie closed them? I remember some guy getting arrested last night, but after that, everything seems a little fuzzy.

My mouth is drier than a barren desert pool, when I try to swallow, only a miniscule amount of saliva can be produced. Ugh, my mouth tastes like the fuzz out of a dryer filter, not that I really know what that tastes like, but you get my meaning, right?

Reaching over, I grab my glasses from the nightstand and slide them on so I can see the time on the clock. It's 11 am. Okay, so not early, but considering I don't remember what time I crawled into bed, it feels like the middle of the night.

Flopping back on my pillows, I close my eyes. My head is banging like a kid is learning to play the drums in my brain. I squeeze my eyes closed hoping whoever was pounding on my door has left, thinking I wasn't home.

As I feel my eyes getting heavy, and sleep creeping in, the fucking pounding starts up again. They are obviously not going to give in. I groan loudly, throw back the bed covers and stumble to my feet. When I try to stretch, I find I'm aching all over, probably from dancing all night. Doing my best not to run into anything as I stumble from my room, I head towards my front door. Using my fists, I wipe the sleep from my eyes and realize I don't remember removing my makeup last night. I probably look like a bloody racoon.

There's nothing I can do about it now, I sigh and open the door. "What the fuck...." I gasp when I see eyes the color of the greenest fields staring back at me.

I watch as his eyes travel down my body, before coming back up to lock onto mine. I hear him murmur, "Betty Boop," in the deepest, sexiest, panty-melting voice I have ever heard.

But, *Betty Boop?* I scrunch up my nose, wondering what the hell he is going on about and glance down. I'm wearing boy shorts in black, and a black singlet with *Betty Boop* on the front. I feel heat creep up my neck at the fact I've answered the door in my underwear, but then I realize, I don't know who he is, or why he is here. Instead of covering up, I stand straight and stare into his eyes. "S.s.sorry." Damn, I stammer when I notice the slight flare to his nose and clear my throat before speaking again. "Can I help you?"

He shakes his head a little, as if he's refocusing, and puts his hand out for me to shake. "Miss, sorry to bother you. My name is Detective Deacon Black, I'm with the New South Wales Police force." He slides his hand into his pocket, draws out a card, and hands it to me.

I take it and look down, as I read I run my finger over his name - Deacon. "Fuck that's a hot name." I think to myself, but when I hear him chuckle, I realize I've spoken the words out loud. The heat in my face which was beginning to fade, returns full force, I know I must be bright red and duck my head to hide my embarrassment.

I clear my throat again before asking, "Would you like to come in?"

"Thank you, Miss ...." He pauses and stares at me for a moment. I realize he is waiting for me to give him my name. *Fuck what the hell is wrong with me.*

"James, my name is Leia James"

Nodding, he squeezes past me. I feel the brush of his arm across my chest, and jolts of electricity consume me, I suck in a breath and attempt to relax. *Fuck I need to get my shit together.* I quickly excuse myself and high-tail it to my bedroom. Elvis is sprawled out on the bed, soft snores escape him and I grumble, wishing I could crawl back under the covers.

I'm trying to figure out what the hell this guy, no correction – Deacon, is doing here. Grabbing my dressing gown from the end of the bed, I throw it on and head to the living room. Deacon is studying photos I have on my television unit.

I head across to the kitchen and flip the kettle on. "Would you like coffee?" My back is turned to him, and I busy myself by pulling two coffee mugs down from the cupboard. I don't wait for his answer before spooning coffee into both.

"I guess, thank you."

He chuckles at my presumption before returning to study the photos. I pause, stiffening, as his deep laugh travels through me, and my body is set on fire with a feeling of euphoria.

"Fuck, what the hell was that?" I whisper to myself and quickly look over my shoulder hoping to hell he didn't hear me. I exhale with relief when I see his back is to me and he's looking at pictures of Georgie, Michael and me.

I take the opportunity to take a good look at the man, fuck, but his ass looks yummy in those jeans. I can't help but notice how big he is, no, not big as in *that* being big, get your mind out of the gutter. I mean big as in tall, broad shouldered, he makes my living room seem so small. I bite my lip, and suppress a moan which is bursting to escape at the sight before me. I turn back to focus on making the coffee, and try to recover from how this man is making me feel. I can only imagine it's what electrocution would feel like. *Fuck get your shit together, Leia.*

My hangover must be worse than I thought because all normal brain functions seem to have deserted me. There is obviously a very good reason why this man is here and I'm sure it's not so I can drool all over him. Maybe he needs my statement from last night, or is he here to arrest me for slapping that jerk? *Fuck!*

~*~

Deacon

Fuck, I have to keep looking at these pictures to keep my mind off what I have wanted to do since the minute she opened her door in her fucking underwear. My body jumped straight into high-alert, protection mode and I wanted to wrap her in my arms, shield her from the world. Who the fuck answers a front door dressed that way? She didn't even ask who was there, I could have been anyone, someone wanting to kill her! *If she was mine, I would redden that ass.*

Calm down, buddy. Fuck, you're here to do a job, so do it! This girl has got my head spinning in a million different directions. I wonder about the possibility of something happening between us, but then, I remember the possessive look in that guy's eyes last night when he wrapped his arm around her and glared at me. I would behave the same way if another man came sniffing around my woman, especially if it was Leia.

Fuck, I didn't think I could get any harder, but then, she spoke and I just about lost it. And, what's the deal with not controlling my mouth? When I muttered *Betty Boop*, I had to look anywhere but at her. I have never met anyone in my life who could throw me off my game before, but one word out of her mouth, and I was like putty in her hands.

I couldn't believe my eyes last night when the dickhead we've been after for the past month, tries to chat this beauty up, and she smacks him straight across the face. It completely blew my mind. I was stunned for a moment, until I saw his hand lifting in response, the possibility of him hitting her was enough to snap me into action. I was furious we couldn't hold the piece of shit on anything, lack of evidence meant we were forced to release him.

Now to the reason I'm here. We found Leia's driver's licence on him, he claimed he found it on the floor, she must have dropped it, and we couldn't prove otherwise. I know I could have sent someone else to drop it off, or posted it to her, but I think I must like torture too much, I had to see her again even if she is with someone else. Honestly? I have no fucking idea why I'm here, I wouldn't have done this for any other woman, but she has this pull to her, I can't seem to resist. I spent the night tossing and turning, and knew I had to see her one more time.

~*~

"Mr Black?"

Her voice ricochets off every nerve ending I have, and I blow out a breath to bring myself under control before I turn around.

"Deacon," I correct when I turn to face her.

I can't stop my eyes from again perusing her body. She's a tiny little thing, barely reaching my chest.

"Deacon, then please call me Leia." She places the coffee on a table between us and gestures for me to take a seat.

The way she says my name, and the blush reddening her cheeks, has me clenching my teeth.

"What can I do for you this morning?" She doesn't lift her eyes from my chest.

I want to reach over and tilt her head until her wine colored eyes lock on mine. But, I resist and tell her why I am here.

"I wanted to return your driver's licence." I bury a hand in my pocket, remove the plastic covered card, and place it on the coffee table. "I also wanted to let you know, the man I arrested last night had it on him, claims you must have dropped it and he picked it up."

I watch as her eyes widen in fear with the knowledge her license was found in the hands of a stranger. A sleazy stranger at that.

"Are you telling me he knows where I live?"

"He claims he didn't look at it and just shoved it in his pocket, I know that's bullshit." I cringe when I curse, and my eyes dart to hers to make sure I haven't offended her.

She shrugs and I breath normally again. "I don't believe he didn't have a chance to look at it and take note of your information, but I needed to make sure you're aware and take proper security measures to protect yourself."

I glance around her small apartment feeling like I have been swept back in time to the 50s. It's obvious she loves retro, and I'd be lying if I didn't say I felt comfortable here.

"I have a dog, he's big and scary." Her words are rushed as if she's suddenly realized, she could be in danger.

I raise my eyebrows and try not to smirk when a small German Shepard puppy strolls out of the hallway. I'm assuming her bedroom must be down there, it's where she appeared from with her dressing gown.

When she notices my raised eyebrows, she looks over her shoulder. "Well shit, he will be big eventually."

I can't help but chuckle, when the puppy comes to me, and starts sniffing my leg, I bend over and scratch under his chin.

"What's his name?" I laugh when he tries to attack my fingers.

"Elvis," Leia says.

The puppy's ears shoot up, he turns and heads straight to her.

"He is certainly a beast," I laugh. "You might want to let your boyfriend know about what has happened, so he doesn't leave you on your own at night. At least until I can get enough evidence to put him away."

I hated having to say that. What I really wanted to do was, tell her she could call me anytime she needs me. *Fuck get your shit together, man! She has a boyfriend and will call him if she ne...* Her next words put a stop to my silent ramblings.

"I don't have a boyfriend." She pauses for a minute before speaking again. "And, I don't need a man to protect me, I can look after myself very well, thank you very much."

Whoa! Stop the movie! Did she just tell me she's single? My mind zeros in on that fact, and I ignore her bravado attitude from a few moments ago, because I'm so fucking happy she's single. I need to leave and clear my head before I do something which may see me end up with a slap across the face, or worse, a knee to the balls.

I stand, not bothering to finish my coffee. "Well, you have my number so if you need anything don't hesitate to call."

I head toward the door.

"Deacon?"

Her voice brings me to a stop and I grip the door handle in my hand.

"Thank you for dropping my licence off to me."

I don't turn around because I'm hard as fuck, and she will definitely notice so, I nod my head and say, "always." Fuck, I clear my throat. "I meant, anytime."

I hear her snort, and then laugh, as I open the door and close it behind me before I say something else stupid. I have never in my life felt so little control over myself, I'm not sure if I'm happy about that fact, but now, I do know - one way or another Leia will be mine.

As I leave Leia's apartment building, I scan the area, taking stock of my surroundings. I notice how quiet the neighbourhood is. Mayfield, overall, isn't a bad area to live in, but like every neighbourhood in Newcastle, well anywhere really, it has its rough spots.

Turning, I glance up to the third floor. I swear I notice a curtain moving against one of the large windows in Leia's place. I swing around when I hear Jim calling out to me.

"Black, you coming or what?" He chuckles as I make my way to the car, open the door and climb in.

"How's Betty Boop this morning?" he asks on another chuckle.

I growl when I recall the sexy as fuck blush which crept over her fair skin. "We need to find something on that motherfucker, I don't have a good feeling about him. Why the fuck would he take her driver's license, it doesn't make any sense at all? He slips date rape drugs to women, why does he keep their licences? As trophies? Or, is there something we're missing. Let's go talk to that piece of shit's ex-girlfriend."

"I'm as confused as you partner."

I grab the file off the dashboard as Jim starts the car, and flick through the pages, checking every piece of information we have gathered on the prick over the past month.

"Don't forget about dinner tonight, if you don't turn up I'm sending Caroline to get you."

"Don't worry, I'll be there. Your wife scares the shit out of me when she's pissed."

Jim and I laugh and he nods his head in agreement.

"You and me both partner, you and me both. I swear the bastards we put away have nothing on my wife."

Chapter Four

Leia

Shit, like that wasn't fucking obvious, he so caught me staring out the window at him. I move away in a hurry, cross to the nightstand, grab my phone off charge and dial Georgie's number.

"Lee Lee, I didn't think I would be hearing from you so early," he laughs.

I roll my eyes and make a beeline for the kitchen to grab a couple of headache tablets, hoping to hell they'll help with this hangover. I shake a couple of pills from the bottle on the bench, grab my now lukewarm coffee, take a mouthful and swallow the tablets down.

"The detective from last night came over to give me my licence back, apparently that jerk from last night, you know the one I slapped, he had it on him."

"How the fuck did he get it?"

"I have no bloody clue; did you leave my clutch unattended?"

"No...." he pauses, obviously thinking back to last night. "Ah shit, I was talking to Michael while you were in the ladies' room, your purse was on the table, maybe he got it then. Shit Lee Lee, I'm sorry."

"It's not your fault, I'm just thankful I got it back."

"Yeah, I guess." He sighs and pauses again. "So, tell me, did Mr. Dark and Dangerous look as good today as he did last night?"

I have the mug to my lips, and I'm about to sip at my coffee when I crack up laughing at his description of Deacon.

"Mr. Dark and Dangerous? Really?" I laugh.

"Fuck yeah, did you not *see* him last night? Fuck me, if I wasn't so in love with my man, I would be all up on him, not that he would notice me, he only has eyes for you my sweet, Lee Lee."

"You must have been seeing things, and even if that was true, he probably ain't thinking that now. I answered the door straight from bed and I'm sure I resembled a zombie from *The Walking Dead.*"

Georgie loses his shit laughing, and he has the kind of laugh that has me losing it along with him. After a few minutes, and a couple of deep breaths, he seems to get himself together enough to talk.

"Ah babygirl, I doubt you looked that bad."

I groan because I swear it was that bad, and not wanting to discuss it further, I quickly change the subject. "You guys still coming over for the game this arvo? I have to get this program finished for Mr. Samson at some point, but I don't think I can get it done today. I'll probably finish it tomorrow when I'm not feeling like I could drink a waterfall and still be this dehydrated."

Laughing at my misery, before gathering himself again, he answers, "yeah, we'll see you later." Before he disconnects the call, I hear him call out to Michael, "Mickey babe, apparently Lee Lee looks like a zombie from *The Walking Dead!*"

I roll my eyes at the pair of them, and disconnect the call before heading to my bedroom. I grab clothes from the closet and head for the shower, hoping it will help me feel less like a zombie and more like a human again. "I swear this shit only ever happens to me," I mumble to my audience – Elvis. He barks and wags his tail as if agreeing with me.

~*~

After the shower, and feeling a little more human than earlier, I throw on my black yoga pants and a basketball jersey. The jersey is probably my favorite item of clothing. I love the Cleveland Cavs and The Golden State Warriors, but couldn't decide which jersey I wanted. So, George and Michael had this one made especially for me. On the front, one side is the Cavs and the other, Golden State. And, because I have a few favorite players on both teams, the back has everyone's number on it. The fact it's one of a kind makes me love it even more. Throwing my long dark hair up into a ponytail, I wrap a white bandana around my head and tie it at the top. I'm now ready for game day. Bring it on!

Heading to the kitchen, I open the fridge, then the pantry and realize I have nothing. I'm like Old Mother Hubbard. I'll have to run to the shops to grab some snacks, we can't watch a game without snacks, and lots of them! Grabbing my purse and keys off the kitchen bench, I head for the door.

I can't get Deacon out of my head, and the way my body reacted just by him being in my space. Opening the door, I'm about to step out into the hall, when I notice a cassette tape on my doormat. I frown and scan up and down the hallway, but don't notice anything out of the ordinary. Weird, who would leave a cassette on my doormat? I crouch down, pick it up and notice the label reads *Dear Leia.* I scan the hallway again and throw the cassette in my purse, I'll investigate it further when I get home. I ensure the door is securely locked, for some reason I feel spooked, and head toward the stairs. I occupy my mind by running through what I need to grab for tonight - chips, beer, oh and I better grab something for dinner.

~*~

Deacon

"Fuck," I mutter at the sight laid out before me. Karly, the ex-girlfriend of that piece of shit, Donald, from last night, is tied to her bed with her throat slit. Written in blood above the headboard it says - 'The Gift'. if it wasn't for her front door being wide open, and on further investigation seeing the lock had been broken, we probably wouldn't have found her.

"Black!" Jim calls out from somewhere else in the house.

I follow the sound of his voice until I locate him in the garage which is attached to the house. Donald is tied to a chair, beaten to a bloody pulp.

I step closer. "Fuck, are those burn marks?" I lean forward to examine the marks, and sure enough, it looks like someone took a blowtorch to different parts of his body. I glance at Jim, he pulls his phone from a pocket and calls it in.

"What the hell are we missing in this case?" I ask when he finishes the call.

"I don't have a clue, but we need to figure this shit out." "You better call your wife and let her know dinner is canceled."

"Fuck," he mumbles.

I can't help but smirk as he dials. Yep, I would rather deal with whoever this sick son of bitch is, than his wife any day.

Jim walks from the garage as he speaks to Caroline. I grab a pair of gloves from my back pocket, pull them on and take a look around the garage. Boxes are upended, the contents scattered. The doors to a cupboard lie open, its contents also now lie on the floor - old blankets and other crap. I'm about to reach out to close the doors when, I notice what looks like a false panel to one side of the cupboard. It would never have been noticed unless someone was trained to look for something like this. I remove the panel, and inside I find a small lock box which I remove from its hiding place. It's not big enough to hold much, probably a wallet, or a couple of sets of keys. Taking it over to the workbench which lines the back wall, I find a screwdriver and pop it open.

"Fuck," I snap out.

"What did you find?" Jim asks. He's finished his call and comes to my side.

"Fuck," he mumbles when he looks into lock box.

There must be about a dozen licences with photos attached to each one, photos which look like they have been taken from a fair distance away. Leia comes straight to mind. This prick had her licence on him, was he going to add it to his collection?

"Do you think whoever did this...." Jim waves his hand around the ransacked garage. "....knows about this?" He points at the box.

"Considering the whole place has been tossed like they were looking for something, and Donald appears to have been tortured, I'm leaning towards yes."

"We need to get back to the station and look into these licences."

I nod in agreement, I know he's right, but right now, all I wanna do is make sure Leia is alright. After gathering up the box, and shoving it into a plastic evidence bag, we make our way back to the front of the house at the exact moment the crime scene truck pulls up. We go over everything with them before jumping in our car and heading back to the station.

"How did Caroline take the news?" I ask as we pull into the underground carpark of the station.

"She understood," Jim says not too convincingly.

"So, you're fucked then?"

He doesn't reply as we get out of the car and I know I'm right.

~*~

Several hours later, after searching each name from the lockbox, we discover each woman, who the licences belonged to, had been raped and murdered over a period of six years. Most worrying? The killer is still on the loose.

We are waiting on forensics on all the cold cases, when Lieutenant Stevenson comes out of his office and throws a tower of files on my desk. I pick up one from the top, and flip through it as Jim wheels his chair over and picks up the next one.

The scene in the photographs, in my file, is identical to the one from this morning. The victims aren't Karly and Donald, but a woman off a licence in the lockbox and I'm guessing, her partner.

I glance at Jim's open file and see an identical set of pictures.

"I'm assuming the other files show the same scene with the woman on the licences in the lock box?" I ask the Lieutenant.

"They call him *The Shadow*," Stevenson nods, and yes, his MO is the same in each case.

"Son of a bitch! Who the fuck calls him *The Shadow*, and why haven't we seen this case before?" Jim asks.

"My thoughts exactly," I think.

"We've had a special task force set up and they have been trying to catch him for over six years. He never leaves a shred of fucking evidence. Every case is exactly the same down to writing *The Gift* in the victim's blood on the wall at the head of the bed." The lieutenant sits before continuing. "After the second murder, the newspapers nicknamed him *The Shadow*. Detectives Jacobs and Ryan headed up the task force and have been working on this from the start. I think it needs some fresh eyes, and due to the circumstances surrounding Donald, it falls in your lap."

I ask, "are you telling me we have a serial killer out there called, *The Shadow*."

"I remember seeing the news articles about him, but it was a while back," Jim says.

I rub the back of my neck. I pride myself on being a sharp detective so how had I missed knowing about this?

"They call him *The Shadow*, because he leaves nothing behind. Nothing – not a fingerprint, a strand of hair, a thread of fabric – nothing! And, no-one has ever seen him," Stevenson says.

I say what Jim must also be thinking, "okay, I get that, but what the fuck does Donald have to do with it? I mean, he's a victim just like the others."

Stevenson shakes his head. "No, I don't think he is. I believe Donald worked with him, and after you guys arrested him last night, *The Shadow* became worried, he may have spilled his guts. I think he got rid of Donald before you could speak with him again."

Jim reaches over and picks up the lockbox, I hear a slight rattle.

"What was that?" I ask reaching for it.

Jim hands it to me. "I removed everything, it shouldn't be rattling." Flipping it open, I take a closer look but don't see anything. I hold it up, give it a shake and the clinking noise is heard again.

"Does the box look bigger on the outside than on the inside?" I ask nobody in particular as I pull a letter opener from my draw. Flipping the box over I notice a small slit on the base. Sliding the blade of the letter opener into a slot, I pop the base open. About a dozen keys fall onto my desk and a single photo.

"Secret compartment, fuck," Jim mumbles.

Picking up the photo, I notice a date from a few weeks ago written on the back. Flipping it over, I feel like I've been sucker punched when I see Leia's beautiful eyes are looking straight at me. I must have been staring longer than I thought, when Stevenson asks, "do you know her?"

It takes all my control, to not say the one word rolling around in my head - MINE. Instead, I clear my throat.

"Yeah, It's the girl from last night Leia James," I say through gritted teeth.

Jim's head jerks up. "The girl from the club?"

"Yes."

"What's the bet, those keys are from the twelve victims, but why is Leia's photo in there?" Jim asks.

I pull my eyes away from the photo, look down at the keys and count them. "There are thirteen keys here," I whisper. A feeling of cold dread envelopes me.

"I'd say you boys better go and check if any of these keys fits Miss James' front door," Stevenson says.

I nod, anxious to get going and check my woman is safe.

Jim gets to his feet with me. Every nerve in my body is on edge at the thought, some sick prick is after my woman. A fierce possessiveness I have never felt before, grips me. I reach for my gun, and slide it into the holster at my hip.

Jim does the same before he slaps my shoulder, and Stevenson returns to his office. "We'll find him."

I nod, acknowledging what he said, but I don't think I'll think clearly until I see for myself that she's okay. I need to protect my woman.

Fuck, when did I start thinking of her as my woman, we have only just met for fuck's sake. It's been less than twenty-four hours, but I can't help claiming her for myself. Images from earlier this morning flash through my mind. Yeah, she's my woman, she just doesn't know it yet.

Chapter Five

Leia

"Lee Lee, it's about to start, get your ass over here girl," Georgie shouts.

I look up at the television in time to see the players take the court. "I'm coming." I grab three beers from the fridge and hurry to the lounge. I place the beers on the table as the whistle blows.

"Perfect timing, baby girl," Georgie smiles at me and I wink back, knowing I had plenty of time. There was no way I was missing the first jump.

"So how did you pull up this morning?" Michael relaxes back on the lounge and takes a sip of his beer.

"Like death." I take a sip of my beer and hold up the bottle "But, this is helping." I laugh and roll my eyes when the boys start chuckling, probably remembering my reference to the walking dead.

We're well into the third quarter of the game, and about my fourth beer, when Stephen Curry throws up a three pointer. I'm cheering loudly when Georgie gets to his feet and heads to the front door. I don't take any notice, but look back at the screen in time to see LeBron James take the ball back down court and slam it in. I jump up, whooping and waving my arms around like a crazy person.

"Shit I can't believe you missed that, Georgie." I stop speaking when I turn and see Deacon and an older gentleman standing at my front door with smirks on their faces. I spin to face Georgie and notice he's biting his lip to stop himself from laughing, but Mickey next to me, can't seem to hold back.

"Well shit." I groan and snap my eyes to Deacon when a deep chuckle bubbles from his mouth, I swear I feel it right to my bones.

Mickey reaches over and grabs the remote to pause the game. God, I love technology. I know they will replay the game later, but why wait until then when we can pause it now?

"How can I help you fine gentleman this afternoon?" I think I sounded a little flirty and suspect I spoke with a bit of a slur. My suspicion is confirmed when Mickey reaches over and grabs my beer.

"No more for you Lee Lee." He chuckles and I feel the heat creep into my cheeks, but I push forward. I mean, how much worse could this get now?

I look back to Deacon when I feel his eyes on me, when I lock eyes with him, I swear my breaths picks up speed. "Wanna join us?" I wave my hand around, trying to break the sudden fog which has settled around us. I must be stuffing this up, as Georgie cracks up laughing. Shit, why did I think things couldn't get worse? It's probably best if I just shut my mouth now. The older gentleman speaks first and I feel a little relieved.

"Sorry, not today Miss James, Maybe another time."

"Babygirl, Michael and I will get things going for dinner while you chat to the police officers."

"Detectives," I blurt out. I'm not sure why I thought I needed to clarify that.

For fuck sake, ground can you just open up now and swallow me whole. I focus on Deacon when he takes a couple of steps towards me, but he must think better of coming closer and stops in his tracks. Fuck the way he's looking at me, it's like he could eat me alive. I feel heat spread through my body. I'm blaming the alcohol for this, because I swear this shit behavior is not normal for me. I think Mickey was right to take the beer away from me. Deacon speaks and breaks into my lust filled brain, I lick my lips at the sudden dryness. His nose flares a little as his eyes track the movement.

"Miss James?"

"Hmmm, yeah?" Fuck, get your shit together! I sneak a glance to the kitchen when I hear the guys laughing at me. "Sorry, what were you saying?" I turn back to Deacon.

An amused smile curls his lips before a serious look crosses his face which has me stiffening a little.

"The man we arrested last night was found murdered this morning."

Yep, that gets my mind back in the conversation. Shit, murdered? But, why are they here? Do they think I did it?

"I didn't do it," I blurt out.

"We are not saying you did, Miss, but we need to ask you a few questions."

"Of course, please take a seat" I wave my hand toward the couch.

~*~

"I'm Detective Jim Barnes." The older gentleman extends his arm and I shake his hand. "You already know my partner, Detective Deacon Black."

I nod my head "Nice to meet you. So, if you're not here to arrest me, what would you like to know?" I take a seat opposite, sit up straight and place my hands in my lap. I feel like I'm back at school and in front of the Principal. *What the hell is wrong with me? Stop acting like an idiot and start acting like the twenty-nine-year woman you are!* I chastise myself.

"The man from last night, had you ever met him before," Deacon asks.

I try to concentrate on his question and not let his voice affect me. "No, never."

"Think hard, you're sure you have never seen him before?" Jim writes something in a notebook he's pulled from his pocket.

"No, I'm sure, not that I know about, anyway." I bite at my nail while I try to think if I have ever seen his face before, but I can't recall him.

Deacon blows out a deep breath and I gaze into his green eyes which seem worried. I'm about to ask what's going on, when Georgie walks over and places his hand on my shoulder. I watch as those green eyes dart to the hand on my shoulder and I notice a slight tick in his hard jaw, he's not happy about it.

"What's going on?" Georgie asks.

"We found a photo of Miss James, dated from two weeks ago, in our search of the dead man's belongings this morning."

"What the fuck?" I glance back and forth between the two detectives, wondering why the hell this guy had a photo of me.

Deacon drags his fingers through his dark hair and rubs the back of his neck. I admire the way the muscles of his arm flex. I shake my head, it's the last thing I should be thinking about right now. Some creep had my photo.... I'm cut off mid thought when Deacon speaks.

"We also found more than a dozen keys with your photo, we need to make sure one of them doesn't fit your front door lock as we suspect."

I gasp, my eyes widen, this shit can't be true. I tremble and shake at the realization, someone had keys to my apartment. I'm pulled into a hard chest I know so well, and Georgie's hand rubs up and down my back as he speaks over my head.

"Do what you have to do." I feel him kiss the top of my head.

I turn to see a frown cross Deacon's face before he stands and heads towards my door. He pulls a key in a plastic baggie from his pocket.

"I'm going to the bathroom," I whisper to Georgie. I take another look as the detectives start trying keys, sprint to my bathroom, slam the door and make it just in time to the toilet before throwing up.

Deacon

Taking a few deep breaths, I control the urge to push the guy away and hold her myself. Fuck! I try to concentrate on the keys, I'm hoping to Christ none of them will fit. The look on her face when she heard about the keys, was enough for me to say fuck it and wrap my arms around her. But, despite the struggle, I remain professional.

I picture how she looked when we first arrived and imagine what it would be like to sit around and watch a game with her. She looks so fucking sexy in her jersey and I picture her wearing only that as I run my hands up her bare legs… Shit, stop! Fucking concentrate on why you're here and what you're doing before the semi your sporting turns to a full blown hard on.

"Are you sure it was Leia in the photo you found?" her friend, I think she called him Georgie, asks from behind me.

"Unfortunately, yes sir, it was," Jim answers as I try a key in the lock.

"Thank fuck," I mumble low so only Jim can hear me.

"I guess that's a no on the keys?" Jim asks quietly from beside me.

I nod, it's good news, but also bad because we have no clue where this extra key belongs. We know it's extra because each of the other keys has a name engraved on one side corresponding to the other victims, this one is blank. After finding the photo, we thought it must belong to Leia. Turning around I look at her friends wondering where Leia is.

"Where did Miss James disappear to?"

"Bathroom," one of the men replies.

I nod and we stand there staring, sizing each other up before Jim speaks, breaking the silence. *What the hell is going on with me today?*

"Will you guys be okay to stay here with her for a couple of days until we can tie up a few loose ends?"

What the fuck, Jim? I glare at him and my stomach squeezes with jealousy at the thought of the two men staying here with her.

I remember what she said this morning about not having a boyfriend and try to relax. Newsflash! It doesn't work, the thought of them being here stings like hell.

"Do you believe she's in danger?" The other man steps forward and wraps an arm around the one called Georgie.

Huh? It's lucky Jim speaks, I've got no fucking words.

"At this point in time we don't know, consider it a precaution."

The men nod before sitting, arms still wrapped around each other, the feeling of jealousy loosens its hold.

"I'm going to need your names for our report so we have a record of this conversation," Jim says flipping his notebook open.

"Sure, I'm Michael Sullavin and this is my partner, George Jamerson."

When it finally registers, the other guy has said *partner*, I blow out the breath I didn't realize I was holding and look towards Georgie. I watch as a smirk pulls at his lips. Fucker, he knew what I'd been thinking when he had her in his arms. Shit, just hearing the men are partners makes me feel a whole lot better. I don't have a problem if you're gay, straight, or even polka-dot, but knowing that these guys won't be trying to hit on my woman while I'm not around has me feeling a lot less edgy.

"We better get going," Jim says and I know he's right.

We have a shit load of stuff to go through, as well as trying to figure out where this key belongs, but I need to see her first. I need to know she's okay.

"Give me a minute." I head in the direction Leia had come from this morning. Walking down the small hallway, I see a light on and a door slightly ajar. I ease it open, step in and find her laying on her bed with her back to the door. I study the curve of her body, wanting nothing more than to go to her, wrap my arms around her, protect her. I'm so captivated by her body, it takes a moment for me to hear the soft sniffs of crying coming from her. Slowly, so as not to give her a fright, I approach the bed and speak softly, "Leia are you okay, sweetheart?"

She rolls over and sits, her wide eyes show everything she is feeling.

Fuck it! Lowering onto the side of the bed, I wrap my arms around her. Her body stiffens at first before she melts against me. Fuck, she feels good in my arms. I breath in the scent of strawberries and it makes my mouth water. Pulling back a little, she gazes up at me. I notice how glassy her eyes are and a tear is trapped in her lashes.

"What's happening here?"

I don't know the answer to her question so, I tell her the truth. "I don't have a fucking clue."

A light chuckle causes her chest to rumble against mine and her tiny fingers grip my shirt tighter.

"I'd like to let this ride out and see what happens." I pull her back into my chest and plant a small kiss to the top of her head.

"Okay," she whispers so low, I barely hear it.

"Okay?"

"Yeah, okay. Every time I've been around you, I feel this weird connection." She blows out a breath and continues before I can reply. "Maybe it's just me, I don't know." She shrugs and leans her forehead against my chest.

I know exactly what she means. Lifting her chin with my finger, I stare into eyes which seem to see straight through me, and everything I was about to say, vanishes from my head. Fuck, she is absolutely breathtaking. Leaning forward, I'm a breath away from her lips. I open my mouth to speak and feel her lips press against mine. I groan and lift my hand to the back of her head, holding her in place as I deepen the kiss. Sweeping my tongue across the seam of her lips, she gasps and I take the opportunity to slip my tongue inside. Wanting, no *needing*, a taste.

Leia moans at the contact and it takes every ounce of control not to push her back on the bed and show her exactly how she is making me feel. Drawing back, I rest my forehead against hers as we catch our breath.

"I have to head back to the station, but remember, if you need me, call. I won't let anything happen to you," I swear.

She nods and runs her tongue across her lips, making me growl, wanting another taste.

Leaning forward, I plant a quick, hard kiss to her lips. When I pull back, our eyes lock and I breath the one word I have been dying to say since I first saw her……

"MINE."

Chapter Six

Leia

Holy shit! I watch as Deacon leaves my bedroom and I can't help but feel the sense of loss. I run fingers across my lips and I swear they're still tingling. I run my tongue across my lips still tasting him and groan. I need more, so much more. The way he just kissed me commanded control and turned my body to butter. My entire body surrendered to him and it was one damn kiss! Never in my life have I reacted that way. When he breathed *Mine* into my mouth, it was like every single cell locked onto that one word and knew it was true.

How is it even possible to think or feel we belong to each other after such a short time? I mean, it's been what, forty-eight hours? We exchanged a handful of words and names and that's it. Oh, and *the kiss* of course. Why can't I stop thinking about what it would be like to be his? Would he push me aside in a couple of months because I'm not open enough? My stomach twists at the thought.

"Lee Lee," Mickey says from my door, pulling me from my thoughts. I frown when I see the worried look on his face.

"Did the keys fit?" I'm almost too scared to hear the answer.

"No, but the detectives said they needed to get back to the station, to try and work out why that man had your photo."

I nod, I'm still trying to get my head around everything that's happened in the last half an hour.

"Georgie almost has dinner ready." Mickey sits next to me.

I nod again, not sure what to say. I m so bloody confused about what is happening - murder, a stranger having my photo, the kiss and the last word Deacon said before he walked out -Mine. What does that even mean?

"Mickey." My voice is hoarse and cracks as I speak. Mickey wraps his arms around me and I rest my head on his chest.

"Leia honey, the detectives know what they're doing. Try not to worry too much. Georgie and I are going to stay here with you for a couple of days."

"No, don't be silly, I'll be fine." I guess there isn't much conviction in my voice because Mickey chuckles lightly and rubs a hand up and down my back.

"That was the most unconvincing statement I have ever heard come out of your mouth.

"There isn't enough room here and I don't want you guys sleeping on the lounge." I watch Elvis trying to jump up on the bed and giggle when he gives up and starts barking at Mickey.

He leans over the side of the bed, picks him up and places him beside us. He snuggles between me and Mickey. I reach down absently and stroke his head as we all lie in silence.

"How about a compromise? Pack a bag for you and Elvis and we'll head to our place where we have room for everyone."

I think that may work. "Okay, thanks," I mumble not ready to get up yet. I roll on my side to face Mickey. "Deacon kissed me and said I was his."

Mickey laughs. "Lee Lee, you could cut the sexual tension with a knife earlier. It doesn't surprise me that he kissed you and said you're his, he's very Alpha."

I'm not sure what to say to that, so I stay silent.

"I saw the way he reacted when Georgie put his hand on your shoulder, I'm sure he wanted to rip it off. Talk about a green-eyed monster. Literally. I mean, I've never seen such green eyes." He laughs and I giggle.

"How do you feel about it?" he asks after a moment.

I'm not sure so I shrug my shoulders. I guess that's not good enough for him because he nudges me in the side with his finger. His and Georgie's signal for 'out with it.'

"I don't know, he kissed me like I was his world. But, how can that be? I literally just met him and each time, I was either drunk or hungover." I pause a minute and think carefully about my next words "Usually I don't give a shit what people think of me, I am who I am and I'm not going to change for anybody, but what if he decides he doesn't like the person I am? What if I can't open up to him? You know what I'm like with men. I have the feeling, if he walked away from me, it would tear my heart out. And, that thought scares the shit out of me. I've only known him for about forty-eight hours and I already feel this weird connection to him. It's like my soul is complete when he's in the same room as me."

"Lee Lee, you can play the 'what if' game all you want, but nobody ever knows what tomorrow might bring. I felt the same when I met Georgie and yes, it scared the shit out of me, but the thought of him with someone else, or not having him in my life at all, hurt like crazy. So, I pushed away the 'what ifs' and took a chance. It's all you can do Babygirl, if you keep holding back because of past failed relationships, you'll miss your one true chance at happiness. Maybe Deacon will be exactly what you need, he'll turn out to be 'the one.' So, stop wallowing about the past, grab onto the future with both hands and ride it out. Everybody has ups and downs, but true strength and happiness comes from pushing and fighting for what you want. If you believe he's your soulmate, then Babygirl, hold on with both hands and never let go."

I think about what he's said and nod my head into his chest. A spike of jealousy hits me square in the chest just thinking about Deacon with someone else. I definitely don't like the thought of that at all. Shit, I have never been jealous over a guy in my life, but thinking about his lips on another woman's, has *my* little green monster rearing its ugly head. When he said I was his, does that make him mine? As in mine only, because I don't think I could share him. I would probably end up getting arrested for murder.

I ditch the thought of committing murder and Deacon touching someone else, and take a few deep breaths before I speak again. I have worked myself into quite a tizzy, I want to find him and make sure we're on the same page. *Yeah, that would turn out well! How about I hold back some of the crazy for at least a week, give him a chance to know me.*

"I forget sometimes, how smart you are." I lift my head and smile, hoping I don't have a crazy, want to murder someone, look in my eyes.

Mickey laughs, he sees it, he knows me too well. "Seriously, I don't say a lot, I usually leave it to Georgie as you know."

We both erupt into laughter, when Georgie has an opinion or something he wants to say, he never shuts up

"But, I watch and listen. I know you have your struggles, we all do, but I'm telling you now, if you let that man walk away after he has claimed you and sealed it with a kiss, you'll be kicking yourself for the rest of your life."

"Dinner's ready," Georgie calls out, ending our conversation.

"Come on Babygirl, we better go eat before Georgie comes in here and yells at us for ignoring him." He leans over and kisses my head making me smile.

Georgie really lucked out with him, he is such a sweet guy and he really loves Georgie. I know he would do anything to make him happy.

Getting to my feet, I place Elvis down on the floor and link arms with Mickey as we head to the living room where we see Georgie has set out the food on the coffee table.

"How you feeling Babygirl?" Georgie asks as he gives me a side hug.

Mickey heads to the fridge and grabs us all a drink.

"Okay, I guess, considering what's going on."

"Well, your Deacon and his partner seem to have things under control so, let's eat and watch the rest of the game." He kisses the side of my head, lets me go and we take a seat on the lounge.

"My Deacon?" My stomach flutters at hearing the words.

Georgie snorts. "Babygirl, whether you want to admit it or not, it's as plain as the nose on your face, that man has laid claim to you without him even having to say a word. Trust me, I know the look *and* the feeling." He smiles lovingly at Michael and I giggle at the pair of them.

They are too cute for words. I change the subject because all this talk about his, and mine, has my body getting all hot and bothered again.

"Okay, let's dig in before this amazing food gets cold."

The boys know my game, but they don't say anything. Michael leans forward and hits play on the remote. I try hard to concentrate on the game, but my head's all over the place, so much has happened in such a short period of time and I need to process it all. I think when I get to George and Michael's place, I might put on some music and make them dance with me.

Deacon

Fuck, the way her body melted into mine when I kissed her has me wanting to head back to her place to finish what we started. Like I told her, I'm not sure what the fuck is happening, but I'm not going to stop until she's mine in every way. I would be a fucking idiot if I walked away from her. But, I know I need to work and get this case solved, I need to know if Leia is involved in some way. The thought of her being hurt has bile bubbling up my throat.

Feeling determined, I flip open the files of each victim on my desk and watch Jim as he pins photos of the victims to a corkboard and attaches a red string leading from the photo to a map which is placed in the center. It gives us a clearer idea of where each murder took place so we can attempt to nail down the specifics of the case. We know each victim has dark hair and they are between the ages of twenty-five and thirty-five. I suck in a breath when Jim pins Leia's photo up.

I'm not a fucking idiot, I know it has to be there, but it hits home a little harder knowing she is on the list and could be in danger. I focus back on the details and facts so I don't completely lose it and manage to get my ass kicked off this case. Studying each file, I concentrate on looking for things that may have been overlooked before the case landed in our laps. I'm not saying the previous detectives are bad at their jobs, but if you have been on a case for a long time, it's easy to miss the smaller details inside the bigger picture. Reading through each case file, I note the victims all lived in different suburbs around Newcastle. I look up when I hear Jim's pissed off voice.

"Son of a bitch," he growls. His back is to me and he's standing in front of the corkboard. I stand and move up beside him. I look at the board and notice the beginnings of what looks like a circle formation where the pins and red strings are attached.

"You have to be fucking kidding me," I snarl, and know exactly what he's thinking. This sick son of bitch isn't done by a long shot, even the murder from this morning fits into the formation. I glance at Leia's photo and notice the blue string attached to it, letting us know she is still alive. Following the blue string confirms my fear, Leia is the next victim in line.

"Fuck," I run my hand over my head and squeeze the back of my neck, trying to relieve some of the tension.

"Black, we will get this piece of shit." Jim places his hand on my shoulder and gives it a squeeze.

"We have to," I grind out between clenched teeth. I just found her, I can't lose her before I have a chance with her.

"Black, we've got this." Jim tries to sound convincing, but I see the worry in his eyes.

I nod and walk back to my desk. I have no words right now and I need to go through these files again. Now, more than ever, I'm determined to find this asshole before he finds Leia. I flop down hard in my chair, Jim takes his seat at his desk, which is bumped up to mine, and I hand him half the files. We dive in and I hope to Christ we find a lead soon.

~*~

"Boys," the voice comes from behind me and I look to Jim, we'd both know that voice anywhere.

I swing my chair around to see Caroline, Jim's wife heading towards us carrying a box. I assume it has food in it for us. She hates when we cancel dinner on her, but she understands the job and doesn't give us too much shit. Well, me, anyway.

"What are you doing here, Love?" Jim stands and heads straight to her. After taking the box and placing it on the desk, he bends and gives her a kiss. Not a small peck to the lips, he grabs the back of her head and kisses her like a devoted husband should.

"You didn't have to bring us dinner, Love," he says after he releases her. I watch as a scowl crosses her face and I know what's coming.

I bite my lip and try not to chuckle as she tells him exactly what she thinks.

"What, I shouldn't have come so you boys can eat crap take away, I don't bloody think so. A good home cooked meal is exactly what you need, I've been cooking all day for tonight so, you will eat it and shut up about it." She finishes by slamming her hands on her hips.

"Yes, dear." Jim bows his head and accepts being put in his place. He may be a detective and take down criminals for a living, but when his wife speaks, he listens.

I can't help it I chuckle at their banter, I mean jeez, when will Jim learn to keep his mouth shut. I shut my mouth when Caroline swings my way and narrows her blue eyes on me.

Caroline is gorgeous, tall with naturally blonde hair and sweet as pie until you piss her off. If you do that, watch out, clear the decks, exit stage left because she's scary as fuck.

"You listen to me, Deacon, and you listen good."

I raise my hands in surrender, like it'll do any good, and I see her lips twitch at the movement. Somehow, she holds onto her laughter and comes after me with both barrels blazing.

"My Jim here...." she thumbs over her shoulder ".....told me you met a real life Betty Boop."

I glare at Jim over her head and narrow my eyes at him. Fuck, I will never hear the end of this. She has been onto me for at least five years to settle down, but I have always put work first and wanted to become a detective. I've never wanted a woman, they didn't fit in my plan, until I met Leia. Plan or no plan, she's all I can think about now.

"Are you listening to me?" Caroline bends forward and gets in my face. I nod, not wanting to admit I didn't hear a word she just said.

"Bullshit," she mumbles and crosses her arms over her chest. "I said, from what Jim has told me, this girl may just be the right one for you. When do I get to meet her?"

"Caroline...." I start, but she cuts me off.

"Don't, Caroline me, I want to meet her and if I think she can put up with your ass, I say marry her."

I death stare Jim again as he steps beside his wife and places the box on my desk.

"Thank you for bringing us dinner, Love. It smells delicious." He wraps his arm around her waist and bends to kiss her temple."

"You're welcome, but don't think I don't know what you are trying to do." She pats his stomach. "Luckily for you, I have to go and pick up Mathew from cadets so, you boys eat your dinner and I'll talk to you later when you get home, honey." She kisses Jim on the cheek and points her manicured finger at me before turning to leave.

I'm glad Jim and Caroline's fifteen-year-old son is sticking with the Army cadets, it will do him good. I watch as she walks out the door and heads towards the elevators before I turn to my partner.

"Why the fuck did you have to tell your wife about Leia, or that I called her Betty Boop? Fuck she's your wife, you know she won't rest until she gets what she wants."

He laughs as he sits and pulls containers from the box and sets them on the table.

"I love my wife and I would lay the world at her feet if I could, but seeing her bitching at you amuses me and maybe you can finally pull your head outta your ass for five seconds and realize there is more to living than this job. You need someone like Leia and I think you would make a good fit so, the only way I could see you doing something about it was to get Caroline involved."

"You're an asshole, you know that." I take the container of mashed potatoes off him,

"I know," he chuckles and reaches for the container in my hands.

"Nope, these are mine. Consider it as pay back for sicking your wife on me."

I don't tell him, before Caroline came in and had her say, I had already told Leia she was mine. And, fuck him, I ain't telling him shit now.

Chapter Seven

Leia

It's been four days since *the kiss* and my head's still spinning I haven't seen Deacon since then either. I thought maybe he'd changed his mind about the whole 'Mine' thing, but then he called me last night wondering where the hell I was because my ass wasn't at home when he came by to check on me (his words not mine). I became pissed at the way he spoke, but when I heard the worry in his voice I chilled, and the worry of wondering if he'd changed his mind quickly vanished from my thoughts. After explaining where I was, I demanded to know where he got my number from because I sure as shit didn't give it to him. Turns out, before he left my place on Saturday, Georgie gave it to him. I was a little annoyed at first, but then I remembered he's a detective and if he really wanted my number he could have found it without too much trouble. So, I gave in and told him he could keep it. Hah, then he says, what I say doesn't matter because he's keeping it anyway. Yep, that got my back up - *big time*, but I like the idea he challenges me and it kinda turns me on. Now if you tell him that, I'll deny it.

I'm heading back home today, I can't handle this house arrest shit any longer. I love Georgie and Mickey and they insist I'm not under house arrest, I believe they honestly think that. They say it's for my own protection, but I still don't know what I'm being protected from. The only thing I know for sure is, some creep had my picture and now said creep is dead.

Deacon informed me last night, they had found a lead which they were going to run down today. I don't see why I can't go home, I need my space, my things. With that thought, I grab my jacket, Elvis' lead and head for the kitchen where Georgie is.

Mickey is setting up for tonight at the bar. Wednesday is student night, I want to get home and have a quick nap before I get ready for tonight. I've finished the new computer program for Mr. Samson, it feels good knowing it's done and I don't have to rush off to the office every day. Now I can work from home again.

"Georgie, I'm heading home to have a nap." I yawn to make my point known and Georgie laughs. For the past couple of nights, we have stayed up late and watched movies. It's been like a long ass slumber party that never ended and I'm bloody exhausted.

"Okay Babygirl, but are you sure you want to move back home today?" he asks for the tenth time this morning.

"If I don't leave now, I'm sure my eyes are literally going to turn into squares with the amount of television we have watched and I swear I have put on ten kilos." I laugh when I see his eyes zero in on my ass.

"Shhhit you....."

"What, I didn't say a word?" He holds his hands up in surrender.

"You don't need to say anything, I know exactly what you're thinking, so that's bad enough."

"Okay Babygirl, go and get some rest, I'll pick your ass up in a few hours." He laughs when I slap him on the arm heading for the front door.

"Smartass," I call out as I step out.

"Yours or mine?" He shouts as I close the front door.

"Douchebag," I mumble as I head towards my red Holden Astra. I run my hand over the roof showing her a little loving before opening the back door and strapping Elvis into his harness. Once that's done, I slide into the front seat, start my baby up and listen to the engine purr to life.

~*~

I wake with a start, something has woken me. Sitting up, I rub my eyes while getting my bearings. I reach over blindly, grab my glasses from the nightstand and slip them on. I glance around the room wondering what the hell woke me. Seeing nothing, I snuggle back down into my blankets, then, Elvis barks. It's probably what woke me in the first place. I glance at the clock and see the time is 1pm, I sigh. I should get out of bed and start getting ready for tonight. Elvis barks again. I groan, throw back the covers and head towards the living room, the direction his bark came from.

I lean over and scratch behind his ear. "What's up, baby?" I hear a faint knock and cross the room to the door. I peer through the peephole and a woman is standing there.

I unlock the door, swing it open and come face to face with a beautiful woman, well not really face to face, she has at least a foot on me, with blonde hair and a sweet smile.

"Can I help you?" I'm wondering if she's at the right door.

"Leia, hi. I'm sorry for just dropping by like this. My name is Caroline, you know my husband Jim Barnes."

I'm a bit taken aback, does she think I'm sleeping with her husband? I frantically try to work out who Jim Barnes is, not easy in my still sleep filled head. Then, the penny drops, she's talking about Detective Barnes - Deacon's partner. A knot of worry settles in my belly when I think something has happened. I'm standing staring, waiting for her to break the bad news, but she quickly reassures me.

"Nothing is wrong, the boys are fine. I came by to talk to you for a moment if it's okay."

I let out the breath I didn't realize I was holding and finally find my voice. "Of course, please come in." I open the door wider and wave my hand towards the couch.

"Would you like a coffee, cold drink?" I finally find my manners and offer.

"A coffee would be lovely, thank you, dear." Caroline takes a seat on the couch while I head to the kitchen and make two coffees. I'm confused as to why she is here, but she seems nice enough. I hope Deacon hasn't sent her here to give me the brush off. I thought he was man enough to do something like that himself. Fuck, what if she *is* here to tell me he doesn't want to see me anymore? What better way to be a coward, send your partner's wife in to do the dirty work and add a woman's touch to it. My stomach summersaults as I pick up both cups and head back to her.

"Thank you." She smiles at me and I try hard not to shout out – 'just get it over with already' - when she takes a sip of coffee and places the cup on the table.

"I'm sorry to drop by unannounced, but I wanted to talk to you."

I nod, waiting to hear the words I dread.

She pauses for a moment, seeming to be choosing her words. I can't take anymore silence and blurt out the first words that pop into my head.

"That fucking coward bastard, he can't even tell me himself he's changed his mind about us." When Caroline's eyes widen in surprise, I realize my mistake and slam my mouth shut. Fuck what did I just do. I close my eyes and wait for her to yell at me for calling Deacon a bastard, but I open my eyes when Caroline does the opposite and bursts out laughing.

"I'm sorry," I say as I laugh with her.

"Oh dear, don't ever be sorry for speaking your mind. I was worried you were a little mouse, but I see now my Jim was right. You are a spitfire and you would certainly give Deacon a run for his money." She reaches over and pats my knee.

"I'm sorry, what?"

"My Jim said you seem to be the sort of woman who doesn't take crap and would give as good as you got. I have to say, when I first arrived I thought, typical, the man got it wrong. My first impression was you are timid and mousey. But, I can see I was wrong and I have to agree with my husband. Please don't tell him though, he'll get a big head and I can't have that at all."

I laugh and nod before agreeing, I won't say a word to him.

"He also said, we should have been sisters because we are beautifully crazy and it's exactly what Deacon needs. Someone who won't back down, but will always have his back no matter what. My gut tells me you're it."

"Um, thank you?"

"Now, my son is having a sleepover at his friend's place tonight and Jim promised me a night out after all the night shifts he's done this week. So, I better get going so I can get ready."

I know I've just met her, but she is really nice and my next words slip out before I can think. "I'm off to The Karaoke Bar tonight, you and your husband should swing by, it would be fun and we can talk some more."

Her eyes light up at my words and I laugh as a huge devilish smile crosses her face. I really like this woman.

"Sounds like a plan, I think my Jim would love it." She winks at me and I have a funny feeling, he may actually hate the idea. "If he doesn't, it will serve him right for all the late nights I've suffered." She takes another sip of coffee and the devilish smile on her face has us both laughing again.

~*~

A few hours later, we sit listening to a couple singing *Paradise by the Dashboard Light* by *Meat Loaf.* I glance over at Caroline and laugh my ass off at her singing to Jim. I watch as a smile touches his lips before he pulls her in and whispers something in her ear. She ducks her head before leaning in and kissing him. They look so much in love, my stomach clenches as I wish I could have a relationship like them.

Caroline is an absolute spitfire and I love her, she is so much fun to be around. She is the sort of person you can't help but like and I don't think I have ever laughed so much. Georgie nudges me, I pull my eyes away from the couple and look at him as he leans in to speak.

"They are such a sweet couple."

"I know, I was just thinking the same thing."

"She's a bloody spitfire, she reminds me so much of you."

I laugh and whisper in his ear, "Caroline told me earlier that Jim said the same thing."

"Put your hands together for that performance of *Paradise by the Dashboard Light*," Mickey says into the microphone.

Everyone in the club claps and I stand, ready for my turn. I wonder, hope, if Deacon will show up. Jim said he had to tie up a few things and then he was heading here, but that was two hours ago so maybe something else came up.

I head towards the stage and the moment I take the Microphone from Mickey, the energy in the room changes. I swing around to find Deacon staring up at me and suck in a breath. He fills the room, a commanding presence of man. I'm drawn into him as ours eyes lock before I slowly peruse his body. Low slung jeans sit on slim hips, a black shirt stretches across his broad, muscled chest. I draw my lip between my teeth and bite down. Fuck, he's sexy.

I step closer to Mickey knowing exactly what song I want to sing. I whisper the title in his ear.

Mickey's eyes dart to where Deacon is leaning against the bar, turns back and winks at me and searches for the song I want. As the track starts, I lift the microphone to my mouth, lock my eyes with his and start singing *I Want that Man* by *Deborah Harry*. Caroline begins howling and going crazy and a small giggle escapes. She's like my soul sister, God I love her crazy ass even though we've only just met.

Deacon stalks towards the stage when it gets to the part about wanting to be kissed from head to toe. I crook my finger at him and sway my hips a little more as he approaches the edge of the stage. I notice his eyes tracking my every movement. The song comes to an end, but before I can bow, I'm lifted into his arms. His mouth hits mine in a hard, possessive kiss that has my body melting into his and begging for more. *Fuck this man can kiss.*

~*~

Deacon

As I drive to The Karaoke Bar, I find myself shaking my head at the shit Caroline has pulled today. You know, it doesn't surprise me, says a lot, doesn't it?

Jim had left me to tie up some loose ends and headed home. I was shocked when he rang me a short time later to let me know what his wife had done and where they were going tonight. I had just finished reading a file on Shelly White - Victim number 2.

I knew I had to take Jim's advice from a couple nights ago and make time for other shit besides work, and if anybody is worth it, it's Leia. After a visit from Caroline, I hope to Christ she hasn't decided I'm not worth the headache. No matter, I'm not walking away from her. I'll prove to her why we belong together, even if it means I have to beg her to give us a shot. Fuck, when did I turn into such a pussy? It's Leia, it has to be, there's no other explanation. Ever since I first clapped eyes on her, my head has been all over the place. It's driving me fucking crazy, but I wouldn't change it for the world. If it takes me forever to prove she belongs with me, then let the games begin. I'm not walking away until I win her heart. Fuck, I reach down and subtly make sure my dick is firmly between my legs because these thoughts are making me think otherwise.

~*~

Pulling up to the curb, I slot the car into an empty space, climb out and head inside. I go straight to the bar and order a drink. I need to get my head together. I turn around to face the stage when a couple stops singing, and fuck me. I notice Leia straight away, she's wearing a tight pair of black jeans and red singlet shirt with matching red heels, her hair flows down her back and I watch as it swings from side to side, caressing the top of her ass. I fist my hands, remembering what it felt like to run my fingers through the silky strands. My eyes zero into the sway of her ass as she steps up onto the stage. Her eyes find mine when she turns, it's like everything else disappears and it's just us. She bends to say something to her friend Michael and then I hear the first beats of the music. Her husky voice sends chills dancing down my spine. *Fuck my woman can sing.*

I take a quick scan of the room and notice everyone staring at *my* woman. I growl, I don't like men leering at what's mine. I look back to the stage as her hips start to sway and her hand taps her thigh to the beat. I can't stand still anymore, I push off the stool and move slowly towards her. I suck in a breath, my cock hardens when she bends her knees, shimmies to the floor and curls her finger, beckoning me to her. Fuck, she is hypnotizing, but I'm well aware of the other men watching this whole performance. It's time I staked my claim so they know to stay the fuck away and also, so she knows she's mine.

Approaching the edge of the stage, she sings the rest of the song with her eyes locked on mine, it settles some of the jealousy flowing through me. When the song finishes, I don't give her a chance to bow before I have her in my arms, and my lips are on hers.

~*~

Pulling back, I rest my forehead against hers. "Fuck, are you trying to start a riot?" I watch the innocent amusement in her eyes and can't help but laugh. She is a fucking handful and fuck if it doesn't draw me in even more.

"Told you she was the one, Deacon," Caroline says laughing as we approach the table where she's sitting with Georgie and Jim.

I growl at the statement causing Leia to laugh.

"Caroline is amazing," Leia sighs happily.

"You've only just met her, babe, you have only seen one side of her, wait until you see the other"

"I heard that, Deacon," Caroline says as Jim pulls her away.

"Come on, Love, dance with me." Caroline giggles and throws herself into her husband's arms.

"They're the sweetest couple," Leia muses as she watches them head to the dance floor.

I glance at my partner and his wife, and have to agree.

"You want sweet, babe?" I whisper in her ear, nip the lobe and feel the shiver race through her body.

She gazes up at me with bright eyes, bites her lip before releasing it, leans up on her toes and breaths into my mouth.

"I just want you." Then, her lips are on mine and I feel it right down to my soul.

Chapter Eight

Leia

Heading from the bar back to our table, I try to work out what the look crossing Deacon's face was all about when Sharon put our beers on the bar. I raised my eyebrow at him, wondering if he wanted to say something, but he shook his head.

We take a seat at the table and Georgie places a hand on my arm, leans over and whispers in my ear, "what are you thinking so hard about, Babygirl?"

I feel Deacon's arm, which was resting on the back of my chair, wrap around me and pull me closer to him. I smile at the possessive move wondering why he is being all caveman, he knows Georgie is gay. I guess he thinks men are men.

Georgie winks at me, he knows what I'm thinking. I answer his question so he doesn't worry, but I really don't want to elaborate right now so, I give him the short answer.

"I'm good, we'll talk about it later." He nods, he's been my friend for a long time and understands it's not something I want to discuss right now. He turns his attention back to Jim. I'm wondering where Caroline has disappeared to when I feel Deacon's hot breath on my neck. He whispers into my ear causing goosebumps to break out across my skin. He feels the bumps and rubs his hand up and down my arm.

"I'm pretty sure Caroline is in the bathroom," he chuckles. "I think she may have had too much to drink."

I giggle, knowing he's probably right. I told her not to do those shots at the bar an hour ago, but she couldn't resist the name of them. And, okay, I may have had a couple with her, don't judge. You would have tried them, I mean who could resist a drink with a name like White Gummy Bear? After two shots each, Sharon explained what was in them - Cherry Vodka, Peach Schnapps, Pineapple juice and a splash of Sprite. No wonder my throat felt like it was on fire! At first, they had a sweet, tart flavor, but then — whammo! They were yummy, but I guess Caroline had one too many.

"I'm going to see if she's okay." I lean over and kiss Deacon's cheek before standing. I feel his hand slide down my side till he reaches my ass and gives it a quick squeeze.

~*~

Making my way to the bathroom, my head feels a little fuzzy and I try to side step my way around the people standing around. But, I walk head first into somebody's back.

"Shit, I'm sorry," I hurriedly apologize when I notice him spill his drink. I look up into his eyes when he turns to face me. They are deep brown and look almost black in the lighting, but that's not what gives me an uneasy feeling and sets my body on instant alert. His eyes seem to narrow a little before softening when they take me in.

"I'm sorry," I repeat.

He begins to say something, but Caroline steps up beside me and loops her arm through mine. The guy looks at her, back at me, winks and turns away.

"He was a bit weird, wasn't he?" Caroline's words are slurred and she starts giggling.

I nod, unsure how to describe the uneasiness I felt from him. Caroline leans into me and I wrap my arm around her waist before she hits the floor. I concentrate on keeping her upright instead of the guy.

"You're such a light weight," I laugh and walk her back to our table.

"Am not." She pauses and laughs again. "Okay, maybe I am, but I haven't had this much fun in a while and I'm really happy."

I laugh at her slurring her words and wonder if she had more shots before she went to the bathroom.

"I'm glad Deacon found you, you guys will make beautiful babies."

My eyes widen at the comment and she laughs harder. "We only just met!"

"Well, I knew my Jim was the one after one look, he's my soulmate, we had Matthew a year later."

"Some people are just lucky."

"When you know, you know, do you know what I mean?" She erupts in laughter and I join her. I pass her off to a now laughing Jim and he wraps his arms around her.

I don't even know if she knows what she just said, or if it even made any sense. I'm guessing in her drunk filled head it does.

Sitting back down, Deacon wraps his arm around me, pulls me into his side and I let the feel of him engulf me.

~*~

About an hour later we say goodnight to everyone, Deacon grabs my hand and entwines his fingers with mine before we head outside. A shiver dances down my spine when he rubs his thumb over the back of my hand. I still don't understand how one simple touch can affect me so intensely. I should probably be scared, but Mickey's words from Saturday run through my head. I relax, knowing he was right. I should push fears from the past back to where they belong. It's time to move forward, maybe those past experiences were getting me ready for the right person.

I look up to Deacon and wonder if everything which has happened to this point in my life, has led me to this moment in time and I'm exactly where I need to be. I smile when he leans down and places a soft kiss to my lips as we come to a stop.

"Fuck, I can't stop kissing you."

I smile wider thinking the same thing. Pulling my eyes away from him, I look to the car we have stopped near. I'm sure my jaw hits the ground as I take in the sight of the slick black '69 Ford Mustang Boss 429. I wipe a hand over my mouth worried I may be drooling, but can you blame me?

"Is this yours?" My voice is all kinds of breathy, but right now I don't care.

"Yeah," he chuckles "It's a ..."

I cut him off because I know exactly what kind of car this is. "It's a '69 Ford Mustang Boss 429"

"I'm impressed. I've had her since I was twenty years old. My old man and me worked on her for hours."

I nod as I continue drooling. Walking to the front of the car, I run my fingers over the hood. Turning away from the black beast, I look back to Deacon. I notice the same look on his face he had earlier when I ordered a beer from the bar. I'm worried I may have scared him off a little because I'm not really a girly girl. I love getting dressed up, wearing makeup and of course heels, but I also love laying around in sweats, watching a game and drinking beer too.

"What?" I ask hesitantly.

He shakes his head. "I've never meet a woman like you before."

"Is that a bad thing?"

"Fuck, babe," he growls and wraps his arms around me. "It's sexy as fuck."

I wrap my arms around his neck and we kiss long and deep. After a moment, he draws back and we are both breathing heavy.

"I can change a tire too," I say.

He chuckles and kisses my nose. "You keep getting better and better."

I smile up at him. "Can you take me for a ride now?" I raise an eyebrow at him when he growls and slaps my ass.

"Get your sexy ass in the car."

I squeal, run around to the passenger side and hop in. Deacon laughs at my excitement as he gets in and puts the key in the ignition.

"You ready, babe?"

"Show me what she's got." I giggle as the engine comes to life.

He presses his foot down on the accelerator and the engine roars, I moan at the sound of sheer power.

"Fuck," I whisper. Deacon looks over at me and I see the hungry look in his eyes, it's like he wants to devour me. I squeeze my legs together at the sudden throbbing in my core. He notices the small movement, a growl rumbles in his throat and his nose flares.

"We need to go." He turns his eyes back on the road. I stare at the flexing muscles in his arm as he switches gears and see the slight tick in his jaw. Summoning every ounce of courage I can, I slide my hand over so it rest on his thigh, I feel the hard muscle flex under my hand.

"Fuck," he mumbles and places his hand on top of mine. He gives it a gentle squeeze and I'm surprised when he leaves his hand there until he has to change gears. As soon as he does, it's back over mine. I drag my nails back and forth, look down and notice the huge bulge in his jeans, I can't help but lick my lips at the sight.

"Fuck it," Deacon curses out.

I'm wondering what's going on when he jerks the car to the side of the dark road. I don't have time to blink before he leans over, grabs the back of my head and his mouth crushes hard against mine. He nips at my lip to gain access and I groan into his mouth. It's like fighting a losing battle when he kisses me, I let him take control, he groans and I suck it down greedily as I run my fingers through his hair, twisting the ends. Pulling back, he rests his head against mine breathing heavy. "We need a flat surface, a bed, anything that doesn't have a gear shift between us."

I giggle at the pained look on his face. "Is it true you can do zero to sixty in 7.1 seconds?" I raise an eyebrow in challenge and watch a smirk tease his lips. He kisses me again, fires up the engine and eases back onto the road.

~*~

Deacon

Holding her hand on my thigh has to be the sweetest torture known to man. Fuck, I lost all sense when I pulled over to the side of the road. I was tempted to take her right then and there, but I don't want any other fucker seeing my girl naked, so I pulled my head out of the fucking clouds and let reason win out.

She absolutely blows my mind, she keeps finding new ways to wow me and I think I've found a unicorn. She blew my mind when she knew what kind of car this is, and when she ran her fingers over the hood, I wanted to bend her over and take what's mine. Shit, concentrate on driving before you have an accident.

I squeeze her hand, not wanting to break the contact and take a few deep breaths. I try to think clearly, but the scent of strawberries hits me, her fingers run small circles on my thigh. I try to think of something to talk about because I'm not sure how much longer my control will hold out.

Cars, that's what we'll talk about because I'm curious to know where she picked up the knowledge about cars or at least this one in particular.

"Where did you learn about cars?" I'm hoping my voice doesn't betray me and give away that I'm trying to think about anything except pulling over again.

"My grandfather." She pauses and peers out the window for a minute before going on. "He used to race in the speedway and the motordrome."

"Sorry, what's a Motordrome?"

"Are you telling me you don't know, or are you testing to see if I do?"

I hear the smile in her voice.

"I have heard about the Speedway before, but not too sure about the Motordrome," I answer honestly.

"The Motordrome is a dirt track about 400m long shaped like a D." I see the smile on her lips like she is remembering something amazing and again she knocks the wind out of me.

"When I was a little girl my mum and dad use to take me every weekend. I still remember the smell and the sounds as the cars raced around and the dirt and mud from the track were thrown onto the crowd when they took the corners. I was so proud my pop was racing and when he won he would drive around with a flag out the window. He'd slow down when he got to me and wave."

I laugh as she sighs and settles back into her seat.

"My dad used to race as well, that's how he met my mom," she laughs.

"What's so funny?" I ask.

"The way my parents met, I used to beg to be told the story over and over again. My mum would go and watch her dad, my pop, race. Sometimes my father would go with his mates and you know those people who walk around at games and sell stuff?"

I nod and she continues.

"They called them, Winfield girls. They would weave in and out of the crowd selling smokes. Anyway, dad was talking with one and when she walked away my mother said something smart to him about chatting the girl up. They didn't know each other from a bar of soap at this point, my father didn't know what to say so he denied chatting up the girl and walked away. So, long story short, my dad wanted to get into racing and one of the older guys who hung out there, introduced him to my pop. Dad had no clue the girl he'd met previously was pop's daughter. Dad ran across mum more often and would shit stir her. My pop found out and basically pinned him to a fence, dad was told to stay away from her. He obviously didn't listen. One thing you didn't do was piss off my pop. The man was as tough as nails and a lot of people were scared shitless of him, all except dad. Being young and stupid, dad's words not mine, he knew my mum was the one for him so he ignored pop's threats. I guess you can say the rest is history. He eventually gained my pop's trust and made my mum fall in love with him. They're soulmates." Her last words have a sad tone and it twists my stomach a little.

"I always dreamed that eventually, I would take my kids there; when I had some, obviously." She laughs and quickly looks out the window. When I glance at her, I picture her round with a baby. No, not a baby - *my* baby. I can't, and don't want to stop the streak of possessiveness which grips me. She would look so sexy….. Leia cuts through my thoughts when she keeps speaking.

"It closed down back in 2002."

"So, your grandfather taught you everything you know about cars?"

"Yeah, between my pop and my father, they made sure I knew most things. So, if my car broke down, I could at least fix it until pop or dad could get to it." She exhales lightly and I think she is going to say more, but she doesn't.

I suspect there is more to all of it, but obviously she doesn't want to talk about it. I pull to the curb in front her apartment building and notice her thoughts are off somewhere else. Leaning over, I plant another kiss to her soft lips, trying to get her mind onto something else. When a small moan slips out, I know I have her attention.

"Are you coming up?"

"Try and stop me." I jump out of the car and head to her door, opening it for her.

"What manners you have kind sir," she giggles and starts to curtsy

I don't say anything, instead I close the door, push her up against the car and devour her lips. I run my hands up her sides and feel the moment she surrenders and gives me the control I desire. Fuck, if it isn't the most powerful feeling in the world.

"Upstairs now," I growl into her mouth.

Chapter Nine

Leia

I barely have a chance to unlock my door before I'm pushed inside and Deacon slams it shut with his foot. Pushing me up against the entry wall, his mouth takes mine in a deep kiss. My body arches into his as he slides his mouth down my neck, hitting the sweet spot with his tongue. I moan when his teeth graze my skin.

My hands slide over his muscled chest, I grip the ends of his shirt between my fingers and drag it over his head. He hisses from between clenched teeth when my nails rake over hard muscle. He wraps his hands under my ass, lifts me and pushes me harder against the wall. My legs lock around his waist. He leans forward and kisses a line across my breasts, goosebumps pebble my skin.

"Fuck, you taste amazing," he growls and slides his tongue along the side my throat.

I tilt my head back and to the side, granting him more access. My tongue darts across my lips to wet them, my mouth is drier than a desert. I moan when his teeth nip my ear and he sucks the lobe into his mouth to sooth the sting. My heart is pounding in anticipation. His hands grip my ass tighter as he crashes his mouth against mine, our tongues tangle, our moans echo around the otherwise quiet room.

Then, we're moving. I'm not sure where the hell he is taking me, I'm lost in his taste and the possessive way he is holding me. Oh, and at this moment, I don't really give a shit either. He has managed to completely mind fuck me in a matter of seconds and I'm just enjoying the ride.

My back hits the soft bed and I feel the cool sheets against my hot skin which is already coated in a light sheen of sweat. The sensation of cool against hot has me arching closer to him. He sucks my bottom lip into his mouth before releasing it with a small pop. When he eases back, I watch as his green eyes seem to darken in the dim light of my bedside lamp.

Reaching down, he plucks at the button of my jeans and I hear the sound of the zipper as it's drawn down. I want to say, he dispensed of them smoothly, but they snagged at my ankles. I burst into laughter when he swears a blue streak, sits up and wrestles them from me.

Then, I feel the heat of his hand as he cups me over the thin fabric of my undies and starts a slow torture with his palm over my aching clit. I moan and lift my hips, wanting more. His free hand grips my hip and pushes it back to the bed. His caressing stops, I whimper at the loss until I feel him slide a finger along the edge of my undies and deep inside me. He hisses when I clench around the deliciously invasive digit.

"You're fucking soaking, baby." He withdraws his finger and sucks it into his mouth.

His groans of complete pleasure cause my breathing to increase in speed, the sound is intoxicating and turns me on even more. I wriggle against the hand still holding my hip, pulling his attention back to me. I know I have it when he rips my undies off in one quick movement and his tongue takes over what his palm was doing a few moments earlier.

My legs tense, I moan and wriggle when he pushes two fingers deep inside and starts stroking my g-spot. Prickles of a rising orgasm overtake my body and I barely hear him speak with my fogged-up head.

"Fuck, your pussy tastes good."

I barely manage to nod, and I hear the deep chuckle bubble from deep within him.

When he blows softly over my sensitive, heated skin, I try to wriggle away. He pins my hips to the bed and kisses up my body taking my shirt with him as he goes. Remembering the scars, I have on my back, I tense, but then I realize, I'm on my back, he won't see them.

Twisting my arms behind me, I undo my bra as he pulls my top the rest of the way off and tosses it behind him. The minute my bra is released I let the straps fall down my arms trying to tease him a little, but I see the hunger in his eyes, remove it and throw it aside. I watch as his eyes devour me. I have the urge to cover up, but I like the way he is looking at me so, I resist.

Leaning forward, he takes my mouth in a toe curling kiss and I slide my leg up against his jeans. Sliding my nails down his chest, I reach the button of his jeans, pop it open and slide the zipper down. Slipping my hand in, I stroke him over his underwear. He groans into my mouth, pulls away and gets to his feet. I see him grab a condom from his back pocket and throw it onto the nightstand.

I focus on Deacon, watching as his jeans hit the floor leaving him only in black boxer briefs. I bite my lip at how fucking sexy he is. He slips the boxers down his legs, rips the condom package open with his teeth and rolls it over his hard cock. I clench at the size of him.

He stalks towards me and I open my legs, inviting him in. He crawls up the bed between them, leans forward, sucking first one, then the other nipple into his mouth. My back arches and I cry out when I feel the head of his cock hit my entrance.

"My pussy," he growls before taking my lips in a deep kiss. He enters me with one hard thrust.

I pull away from the kiss, throw my head back and cry out.

"Fuck, baby," Deacon growls as he thrusts in and out of me, tangles his fingers in my hair, leans down and sucks my neck.

"Yes," I pant, pushing into him, matching his thrusts. Bringing my legs up, I lock my ankles over his back. I drag my nails over his skin and feel the light sheen of sweat. His muscles flex as he leans into my touch.

"Just there," I pant. "Harder!" I shout as Deacon groans, I feel the rumble vibrate through my body as he slams into me again and again.

Rotating his hips, he hits where I need it. I groan out his name as my legs tense up and pure ecstasy erupts throughout my body.

I breathe heavy, attempting to catch my breath when Deacon leans back and grabs my hips. He slams into me twice, throws his head back and roars my name as he empties into me. Small tremors course through me and another orgasm slams into me.

I hum when I feel his lips on mine, my muscles have dissolved into jelly, I couldn't move even if I wanted to. I open my eyes when his deep chuckle breaths through the sex fog in my head.

"Can we do that again?" I ask breathlessly.

"Babe, anything for you." He chuckles and stares at me as if I've just asked him the most ridiculous question ever asked. He disposes of the used condom, rolls on a new one, thrusts back inside, and we're ready for round two.

~*~

Deacon

You know the feeling you get when you suspect you're being watched? I crack an eye open and notice Elvis sitting beside me on the bed. He's staring directly at me and tilts his head to one side. I scratch under his chin and I guess that earns me his approval, he moves forward and starts licking my face.

"Down boy." I try to move my face away, but he is a persistent little puppy and I chuckle at his excitement. I look over to where Leia was lying, but her side of the bed is empty. Patting Elvis' head, I try to get him to calm down. Sitting up, I search the floor for my jeans. When I spot them, I climb from the bed and pull them on, leaving the button undone. I head to the bathroom and my mind replays the night before.

After taking her the second time, I'd headed to the bathroom to clean up and when I returned, she had her top back on.

"What's wrong?" I ask.

She looked at the bedcover and shrugged which set me on alert straight away. I moved to where she sat, pulled her into my arms and lifted her chin so I could see into her eyes.

"Babe, what happened between the time I went to the bathroom and came back? Why do you have your top on?"

"Nothing happened, I was just a bit chilly."

I knew she wasn't telling me the truth, but I didn't push her. I may not have known her for long, but I worked out pretty quickly, if you push her, she'll push back. I wouldn't get an answer anyway and she'd be angry. I laid her back down and worship her body all over again. I can't seem to get enough of her, everything about her is addictive. But before we go any further I need to know what she is hiding from me.

When she fell asleep in my arms last night, I rubbed my hand up and down her back wondering what she was hiding. I felt something through her shirt and stilled. Welts? Fuck. Now I know, we definitely need to talk. I left it alone last night, but today is a different story, I didn't become a detective because I was shit at my job, either way I *will* find out.

~*~

I pad out to the living room and stop short at the doorway, lean my shoulder against the frame and cross my arms over my bare chest. I watch my woman dancing around the living room in her underwear to *How Do You Do It* by *Gerry and The Pacemakers*. I smile, remembering my mum use to play this song all the time and she drove my father and I nuts with it. I watch the way she moves her body and find myself hypnotized. The song comes to an end and I clear my throat so as not to scare her. She swings around and sees me, a smile spreads across her face. I picture waking up to this every morning. I study her face and notice the smile doesn't quite reach her eyes. Something is wrong, why does she need to fake a smile around me?

I move slowly towards her, wrap my arms around her waist and bend to give her a kiss. Pulling back, I watch as her eyes flutter open.

"Babe, I think we need to talk." I regret the words as soon as they're out of my mouth and I feel her turn rigid, she pushes from my hold, heads to the television cabinet and turns off her iPod. "Leia."

She holds her hand up to stop me talking while she stands with her back to me for a moment. She blows out a breath and turns to face me. I notice every emotion is gone from her face and when she speaks, her voice is flat, lifeless.

"What's up?"

"First, don't do that!"

"Do what?"

"Speak with no emotion."

"Well, if you're going to say you're done with me, you know where the door is, don't let me stop you."

What in the actual fuck did she just say to me? I feel myself getting pissed at the dismissal and the nonchalant way she waved towards the door. Is she seriously dismissing me? "What the fuck do you mean if I'm done with you? I thought I'd made this shit clear to you, but I guess you need a reminder. You're mine, and when I say – MINE, I mean I ain't going anywhere and I'm not going to let you push me away because you're scared. And you are, aren't you Leia?"

"What?"

"You're scared because of something that happened in the past."

"Well, I just thought..." she hesitates, but I don't say anything because she needs to finish what she was saying. "You know." She waves her hand around.

"Nope, not a fucking clue."

"I thought you were changing your mind and ending this..." She waves her hand between us and I'm fucking stunned. How the fuck did she get that from me saying we needed to talk?

"All I said was, we needed to talk. For all you know, I might have been wanting to discuss plans for tonight because I have to head to the station soon."

"Oh okay, sorry." She starts to walk past me, but I grab her arm. Not hard, just enough to get her to stop because we haven't finished here.

"Babe, why would you think I wanted to end things?"

She shrugs, but that's not good enough for me. I think she realizes I'm not satisfied with her answer after a couple of minutes of silence.

"Look, the last two boyfriends I had said we needed to talk before they broke up with me. I guess I hear those words and automatically my brain clicks to *I'm breaking up with you*."

I take a few deep breaths, I don't want to hear about her with other guys, but I understand now why she jumped to that conclusion.

"Okay, come here."

Leia steps closer and I take her hands. "First, I get it, but I don't want to hear about other men. Especially those who have kissed your lips or looked into your eyes. Eyes that seem to be able to see deep inside me."

Her eyes widen, but when she opens her mouth to speak, I continue.

"Second, I'm not leaving you, *ever*. And, you're sure as shit never getting rid of me. Sorry baby, this is a done deal so, I think you need to work it out in your head so we don't have to have this same conversation again, understand?" I raise an eyebrow at her and she nods, but I want words. I want to know she understands what she is agreeing to.

"One day you'll wear my ring and then, when the time is right, we'll have those kids you spoke about wanting last night. Understand me now?"

She sucks in a deep breath and leans up to kiss me, but I pull back waiting for the words. I guess she sees what I'm waiting for

"Okay Deacon, if you really want me, I guess I can live with that." She giggles as I sweep down and take her lips in a possessive kiss leaving her with no doubt as to who she belongs to.

"I have to get to the station, but when I get back here tonight, we *are* going to talk. I understand there are things you probably don't want to talk about, but we'll work it out together. I'll give you the time you need, but babe this is for life so, I want to be the person you can talk to when something's wrong."

<h1 style="text-align: center">Chapter Ten</h1>

Leia

It's been a few hours since Deacon headed to the station and my lips still tingle from the kiss he planted on me before he left. I felt it deep in my bones, it was one of those kisses you read about in romance novels, the type that curls your toes and causes your legs to shake. I was still trying to catch my breath after he left, hot damn my man can kiss. As I head for my bedroom, heat pools at my core just thinking about it.

I sit on the bed and pull out my laptop, I might as well try and get some work done while I wait for him to finish up for the day. I grab my handbag from the floor and rummage through it for my USB stick which has the new program I need to work on. Not finding it, I tip my bag upside down and let the contents spill onto the bed. I find the recalcitrant USB, plug it into my computer and wait for the file to load up.

While I wait, I head to the kitchen for a cola and check on Elvis. He's stretched out on the lounge snoring his head off. I smile at his cuteness and head back to the bedroom. As I approach the bed, I catch sight of the tape I'd received a few days ago. I'd completely forgotten about it.

I set the cola on my nightstand and flip the cassette over in my hand. The label 'Dear Leia' catches me eye. Curiosity gets the better of me, I pull a box from under the bed that I throw random stuff in. Opening the box, I grab my old school *Walkman*, check it has batteries and climb back onto the bed. I pop the tape in, slide on my headphones and press play. At first there's nothing but static, then, what sounds like heavy breathing starts. I'm about to hit stop when a quiet, whispered raspy voice comes through the headphones. It sends chills down my spine and the hairs on the back of my neck stand on end. I want to stop listening, push the stop button, but the voice has me intrigued, terrified and I'm frozen in place.

"What a precious little gift you are, so much beauty. Do you feel me watching you through the shadows, knowing at any minute I could take you away and nobody will even notice? Your voice entrances me, I know you're my next perfect treasure, my next perfect gift."

There's an eerie silence, I think the tape has finished, but then he speaks again and I feel my blood run cold.

"No-one can save you now, no-one can stop me from getting to you.

See you soon, my sweet little gift."

Pushing the headphones off my head, I push back against the headboard and hug my knees to my chest. I glance around the room, I can't help the feeling of being watched. I know I'm the only one here, but I can feel it.

"Elvis," I call out with a shaky voice. I hear him padding down the small hallway, his nails clicking on the hardwood floor. When he comes to the side of the bed, tilts his head and looks at me curiously, I reach down and scoop him up. I place him in my lap and notice how badly my hands are shaking. I need to call Deacon, so he can do something about this tape. I'm not sure if it's connected to the case he's working on, but it's strange how it turned up the day that creep was murdered. I try to flex my hands to stop them shaking but it's no use, grabbing my phone from the nightstand, I dial the number Deacon gave me. I lift the phone to my ear and listen to it ring.

~*~

"Babe," he breaths into the phone. He sounds out of breath, like he's had to run for the phone.

"Deacon...." I can't stop my voice from breaking as tears form in my eyes.

"Babe, what's wrong?" he growls down the phone, I hear the worry, almost panic in his voice.

"Where are you?" he asks when I don't answer him.

"I'm at home," I sniffle. I try to sound normal because this could be nothing and I'm bothering him for no reason. I fail and the tears start to fall.

"I'm fine now, I'm sorry I called."

"You're not fine, you're crying. Tell me what the fuck happened."

I roll my eyes at the command in his voice, but I guess I owe him an explanation after my mild meltdown. I wipe my eyes, sniffle again and manage to speak in coherent sentences. "I found a cassette tape on my doormat the other day, I'd forgotten about it until a few minutes ago when I found it in my purse. I played it and I'm scared." I don't want to worry him while he's working, but I am fucking scared.

"I'll be there in twenty," he says and ends the call.

Well fuck, that went well. Not! I hope he doesn't get mad when he realizes I've probably over-reacted.

I pat Elvis on the head, he tries to nip at my fingers making me giggle. The *Walkman*, at the end of my bed seems to mock me. I rub my arms as ominous chills snake through me. *I'm just overreacting. It's a tape for fuck sake, nobody is here, everything is fine.*

I repeat the words in my head on a continuous loop, all the while feeling it's a long way from the truth.

Deacon

"Jim, we need to get to Leia's place," I call out as I shove my phone in a pocket, reach for my gun and slide it into my holster.

He appears from the lieutenant's office with a worried look on his face. We had just found another lead before Leia called and he was informing the boss, but that shit can wait. I need to get to my woman, now!

"What's happened?" He grabs his gun from a desk drawer.

"She found a cassette tape on her doormat."

Jim's eyes widen in shock and I'm instantly on alert. He moves to one of the evidence boxes lined up against the wall, one I haven't examined yet. He bends down, grabs the box and brings it to my desk. He opens it I feel like time slows down when he pulls out an evidence bag filled with cassette tapes.

My stomach somersaults as I glance between him and the bag.

"Fuck," I spit through clenched teeth.

"Son of a bitch," he snarls at the same time.

"We need to go now!" I shout at him as I grab my jacket from the back of my chair.

I sprint towards the elevators with Jim hot on my heels.

The doors of the elevator whoosh open and we step inside. I hit the button for the basement where our car is parked.

Jim turns to face me. "This is the plan - we'll grab your girl, make sure she's safe and secure and run up the new lead with the locksmiths. I can't believe we missed it before."

I know he's trying to calm my ass down by getting my mind back on the case, but fuck, I know I won't be calm until I hold her in my arms. I nod, watching as the floor numbers light up as we descend. It feels like we're standing, waiting, for hours when in reality it's less than a minute — too long as far as I'm concerned. I'm tempted to stop the car and use the emergency stairs, but remember they're closed off for maintenance or some shit. I feel frustrated and run my hand across the back my neck, trying to relieve some of the tension. Finally, the fucking doors open and we can step out.

~*~

We race to where Jim's car is parked, jump in and he hits the road. My heart is pounding out of control when I recall how Leia broke down on the phone. I need to get to her, take her in my arms and never let go.

It's the longest fifteen minutes of my life before Jim pulls alongside the curb in front of Leia's apartment building. I don't wait for the car to stop before I'm jumping out and taking the stairs two at a time, needing to get to her.

When I set foot on the third floor, my eyes scan the hallway and I have my gun at the ready. I bang my hand against the door of Leia's apartment, all the time checking that no-one has been hiding from sight. I don't hear anything in the apartment and lift my leg, ready to kick the door down, when Jim arrives to join me and Leia opens the door. She throws herself into my arms.

I take a deep breath and calm myself down. She's okay, she's in your arms, I repeat to myself until I feel myself calm. Keeping one arm around her, I holster my gun and finally take a good look at her to make sure she's not hurt. That's when I realize what she's wearing, or *not* wearing. I glance at Jim, but he's busy checking the hallway. Thank fuck!

Pulling her close against me, I breathe in her scent. "I've got you, babe." I kiss the top of her head and she nods into my chest.

"Come on, babe, let's get you inside." She nods but refuses to let go. I sweep her into my arms and carry her inside. Jim follows and shuts the door behind him.

I take a seat on the couch, pull her onto my lap and cover her with a crocheted blanket from over the back of the seat. "Tell me what happened, babe?"

"It's in my *Walkman*."

"On my bed."

Jim stands from the chair opposite. "Jim is going to go get it, okay?" She doesn't answer, but gazes up at me through tear-filled eyes and nods. I hold her close against my chest while Jim heads for her bedroom.

"I'm sorry."

"What are you sorry for, babe?"

"For calling you and making you worry about nothing."

"Babe, you never have to apologize for calling me, especially when some asshole scares you. I want you to call me."

She looks up and locks eyes with me, I guess she can see the truth in my words because she relaxes a little more in my arms. Did she think I'd be mad at her? That's a discussion for later. I would never be mad at her for being scared.

Jim clears his throat and I look to where he's standing in the doorway. I notice he has headphones on and a pissed off look on his face. I feel the anger spike in me when I understand - he's pissed because it's the same as the tapes we have in evidence. Fuck!

"Babe, I need to bring you down to the station." I lean forward, kiss her forehead and whisper, "I need you to go and put some clothes on."

It's then she realizes, she is dressed only in her underwear and a blush hits her cheeks. She knows now why I was quick to cover her with the blanket.

She glances shyly at Jim but he's not paying her any attention. Thank fuck, because he's my best friend and partner and I didn't want to have to beat his ass for looking at my woman when she's only half dressed. I know he's devoted to Caroline, but I still can't stop the jealousy coursing through me.

Leia starts to stand but I shake my head and stand with her in my arms. "Give us five," I tell Jim before heading to the bedroom with my girl in my arms.

He nods and wraps the cord of the headphones around the *Walkman*.

Chapter Eleven

Leia

After throwing on a pair of jeans and a black off the shoulder shirt, I throw my hair up in a messy bun on top of my head. I turn away from the mirror and watch as Deacon grabs an overnight bag from the top shelf of my closet. He pulls random clothes out and shoves them in said bag I must have given him a strange look because he doesn't stop what he's doing, he simply raises an eyebrow and states, "you're not staying here."

"I know. I was going to call Georgie, ask him to meet me at the station and then go back to his place."

"Not happening." His growl ricochets through my body. He crosses to my chest of drawers and pulls open the top one – my underwear drawer!

What in the actual fuck? I jump up, push the drawer shut with my hip, slam my fists on my hips and glare up at him. When I see the worry swimming in his eyes, my anger deflates a notch or two. I soften my voice, I've worried him enough for one day.

"I'm fine and Georgie will look after me." I place my hands on his face and feel the prickle of his five o'clock shadow under my palms as I reassure him. Placing his hands over mine, he leans down and kisses my lips so softly, it's as if a feather has brushed my lips. I close my eyes as tingles shoot through my body and goosebumps break out over my skin.

"I know, babe, but how am I supposed to see you dancing around my living room wearing these if you're not there?"

At his words, my eyes flutter open and I see my red lace panties hanging from his fingers. Well I guess he has a point, but I think I have interfered with his life and work enough for one day.

"What about Elvis?"

"Really, babe? You think we wouldn't take Elvis?" He lifts an eyebrow at me.

I know it was a lame attempt at an excuse, but thinking about being in his space has me all mixed up.

"Stop fighting this, stop making excuses and let it happen." He returns to packing my bag.

~*~

It's like a whirlwind of activity surrounds me when we reach the station, I'm still trying to believe this is actually happening. I'm guided to an interview room - gray walls, a table in the middle with chairs around it and a large, what I assume to be, double sided mirrored window on the wall. Hmmm, their interior decorating sucks.

I expect Deacon to be on the other side of the window after hearing Jim tell him it was best if he didn't come in. He warned him, he could get kicked off the case if their Lieutenant found out he sat in with us. Deacon wasn't happy about it, I could see the tick in his jaw thumping, but he nodded and disappeared through another door where I assume is where he will watch everything happening.

After escorting me into the room, Jim leaves to grab us a coffee. I can't help the feeling which settles over me that this shit is worse than I originally thought.

Tapping my nails against the table, I try to think if there's been anything else out of the ordinary lately, but nothing comes to mind. I'm snapped out of my thoughts when Jim enters the room juggling two coffees and a file lodged under his arm. I stand to close the door, but he sticks his foot out and closes it.

"Here you go." He passes me one of the cups before taking the seat in front of me. After pulling a notebook from his pocket, he opens the file he'd been carrying.

"Thank you." I take a sip and must pull a weird face because Jim chuckles at me.

"Yeah, the coffee around here *is* that good"

"It's enough to put hairs on my chest, Jim." He chuckles again before a serious look crosses his face.

"So, can you run me through what happened?"

"It was the morning you first showed up at my place to let me know the creep who tried to grope me had been murdered. After you left, I needed to run to the shops and when I was leaving my apartment I found the tape on the doormat."

"That long ago?" Jim asks.

"Yeah, I picked it up and threw it in my purse then, I forgot about it. This morning I was looking for my USB stick so I could get some work done and it fell out of my bag. Curiosity got the better of me and I wanted to know what was on it. Knowing what I do now, I wish I'd never listened to it." I shudder when I remember the scratchy voice and rub my arms to ward off the chill.

"No one can save you now and no one can stop me from getting to you.

See you soon my sweet little gift"

Those words will stay in my fucking head until the asshole is caught.

"Did you recognize the voice?" Jim asks, breaking into my thoughts. I think about his question, but for the life of me, I don't have a bloody clue.

"No, I've never heard it before."

"Have you noticed anything else unusual lately?"

"I was thinking about this earlier, but there's been nothing out of the ordinary." I squeeze my hands together to stop me from shaking. I look up into Jim's eyes when he places his hand on top of mine and speaks softly to me, "we will find this guy, Leia, I promise you."

I nod, not trusting my voice right now as I'm about to burst into tears. I close my eyes, allowing the warmth of Jim's hand and his words, calm me.

I open my eyes when I hear Deacon's voice, he's standing by the door and waits as Jim leaves the room. A single tear slides down my cheek and then I'm out of the chair, in his arms and hard up against his chest. His hand rubs up and down my back, soothingly, and I break. Everything I've been holding in since I heard the tape, rushes forth. I don't even care if he feels the scars on my back. I need to let go, I sniff in an attempt to slow the tears, lean back and gaze into his eyes. I repeat the words he said to me this morning. "This is for life?" I whisper

"Yeah, babe, for life." He nods and relaxes, he must see in my eyes, I'm ready to let him in.

~*~

Deacon

Her eyes clear, the minute she realizes I was telling her the truth this morning, this is for life. Her and I, us, for eternity. I relax, knowing she is with me one hundred percent. After she fills out a few forms and signs her statement, we leave to pick up Elvis from her place so I can take them to mine. Fuck, what will it be like to wake up with her every day and see her in my space.

My dick pushes against the zipper of my pants at the thought. Fuck, I need to get my shit together. Taking my eyes off the road for a second, I glance across and see a faraway look on her face as she stares through the window at the passing scenery. I doubt she is taking anything in, her worry is obvious. Her hand is on my thigh and her fingers absently rub small circles there. It still surprises me, after knowing this woman for such a short time, one simple touch can have me wanting to lay my world at her feet.

I need a distraction from my thoughts so, I reach over and turn the radio on, turning up the volume a little. *The Wanderer* by *Dion* starts to play and I tap my fingers on the steering wheel to the beat. I focus on the road, but Leia's voice singing along to the radio, hits me straight in the chest. I suck in a sharp breath as her voice travels straight to my dick. Fuck, I ease my foot down on the accelerator and increase my speed, careful to stay under the limit. I see her apartment building in the distance and breathe a sigh of relief. I'm not sure how much of this I can take. The combination of her sweet smell, and her voice, has my cock aching in my pants. I'm rapidly coming to the conclusion that this will be a perpetual state every time I'm near her.

~*~

Entwining my fingers with hers as we make our way up the steps to her apartment, it dawns on me, apart from singing in the car to the radio, she's been pretty quiet since leaving the station. When we reach the second floor, I pull her to a stop, wrap my arms around her waist and wait for her to look into my eyes. She gazes up at me and my heart aches for her. I want to kill the sonofabitch who has scared her.

"Babe, we are going to work this out, okay?"

"I know, so much has happened over the past five days and I guess I'm just trying to work it all out in my head"

I nod. I get it, but fuck, I wish I knew how to help her. I bend down and plant a soft kiss to her lips. When I try to step back, she wraps her arms around my neck and slides her tongue across my bottom lip. She wants me to open and let her in. I'm more than happy to give her what she wants. I slide a hand up her back, tangle my fingers in her hair and hold her in place while I deepen the kiss until we're both breathless. Pulling back after a moment, I rest my forehead against hers. Before I lose complete control and take her hard up against the nearest wall, I turn us both towards the stairs and we make our way up to her floor.

Emerging onto her floor we head towards her apartment. I stop dead in my tracks when I notice her lock has been busted in and her door is ajar. Fuck! I push Leia against the wall, pull the gun from my holster and bring a finger to my lips when she opens her mouth to say something. I tilt my head towards her door.

When she catches on and notes the state of her door, her eyes widen. Her lower lip trembles, she wraps her fist in my shirt and whispers, "Elvis!"

Shit. Shit. Shit. I nod before whispering to stay put. Aiming my gun, I scan my surroundings as I approach the door. I ease it open slowly and peek around the door jam. I don't see anything, but keep the gun raised in front of me as I enter the apartment and look around. When I open the door to the bedroom. Elvis hurtles towards me. I gather him into my arms and pet his head.

"Hey little guy, your mumma is worried about you." I head back to the living room and take another quick look around. Satisfied no-one is here, I head back to Leia who is still waiting for me outside in the hallway. The moment she sees me tears start to fall. She takes Elvis from my arms and hugs him close to her chest. Seeing her tears about breaks my heart in two. Fuck, when I find this prick, I don't think he'll make it to a jail cell. No, this prick deserves a fucking body bag.

Chapter Twelve

Leia

Deacon pulls the car to a stop outside a beautiful old house. I look around, the street is quiet, the houses all similar in style. Old wrought iron fencing, old style molding surrounds the large front windows. A smile graces my lips for what feels like the first time today, I'm excited to see the inside of the home. Before Deacon can open my door, I climb from the car and wait for him on the footpath. I feel like I've stepped back in time and I love it.

"It's not much, but it's home," Deacon says softly from beside me. His arms wrap around my waist as I stand taking in every tiny detail of the front yard.

"It's beautiful." My voice is breathy, I gaze into his eyes and he looks as if he's trying to figure something out. "What?" I ask when he keeps staring at me.

He leans over and kisses me softly. "You're beautiful," he murmurs over my lips.

Oh, what this man makes me feel. "Can we go in now?" I bounce a little on the balls on my feet and he chuckles.

He extends an arm towards the house. "After you, babe." He guides me forward with a hand placed on my lower back.

Fuck, all I want to do right now is jump him. I know there is a lot going on right now, but I can't help it, he has the ability to send every cell in my body berserk. Running up the steps to the front door, I swing around and wait for him to unlock the door.

I take two tentative steps into the entryway. I gasp at the beauty of it all. High ceilings, beautiful crown molding etched into the ceiling, it's breathtaking. The warm colors on the walls give it a homey feel. I haven't seen the rest of the house yet, but I know it's going to be stunning if the entryway has me feeling this way. Walking along the hall we come to a doorway and I gasp. Deacon chuckles behind me, but I ignore him, and my traitorous body, as the sound travels up and down my spine. I take in the scene before me.

Polished hardwood floors spread through the house inviting you to explore. The living room has an old fireplace in the corner with a mantelpiece. I notice a few photos sitting on top and think I'll take a look at them later. Comfy looking brown leather couches front up to a wooden coffee table. On the wall above a wooden lowboy cabinet hangs a large flat screen television.

The room is part of a large open-plan space and I pass the old wooden table in what is the dining area. The kitchen has black granite counter tops and stainless-steel appliances which sparkle.

I'm in absolute awe, the combination of modern and old are perfect together. The place is so inviting, it's like my dream home.

"Are we just going to stand here all day?" Deacon asks.

"I'm sorry, but this place is beautiful." I feel like beautiful isn't a strong enough word to describe this place, but it's all I can come up with at the moment. I look up and notice him looking around as if he's trying to see it the way I do.

"I bought this place about seven years ago, Jim and I have been renovating it since. Caroline designed the kitchen and the bedrooms upstairs because apparently it needed a woman's touch or some shit like that." He shakes his head, but he's smiling so he mustn't mind Caroline taking over in the design department.

Then, it hits me, does it mean no woman has ever lived here? A flutter develops in my belly at how good it makes me feel. I berate myself for being so silly, but I can't help it, I love the thought that no woman has shared his home.

"Come on, babe, I'll show you upstairs."

The quick glance at his watch tells me he needs to get back to the station. I was so captivated by his home, I temporarily forgot everything that happened this morning, now it all comes flooding back. Shit, someone left me that tape and broke into my home! Deacon's arms wrap around me, and I notice I'm shaking. I turn in his arms and wrap my arms around his waist, gripping the back of his shirt. I draw on my man's strength until I calm down.

"Babe, everything is going to be okay." He places fingers under my chin, tilts my head back so I'm looking into his eyes.

I nod. "I'll have to change my locks." I sigh and see his eyes widen before he looks off into space, as if in deep thought.

Appearing to shake it off, he takes my hand and leads me upstairs. I run my hand over the carved wooden banister. Deacon shows me into each room, I concentrate on taking everything in.

Wow! If I thought downstairs was amazing, the second floor is bloody spectacular. There's a beautiful old bathroom with a clawfoot tub that has me drooling. Two guest bedrooms, an office and the main bedroom with a picture window overlooking a beautiful manicured backyard. I can't help imagining watching our children playing while I sit under the small pergola with a cup of coffee while Deacon strikes up the barbeque. I shake my head at the image. I mean, really! I've only just met Deacon and it seems like my crazy ass has already moved in and I'm about to push out a bunch of kids. I wonder if they would have the same green eyes as him. *Fuck, get your shit together before you start blurting this shit out and really scare the shit out of him!*

"Babe," Deacon speaks loudly and I swing around to face him. "Wow, you were really zoned out, what were you thinking about?"

I shake my head, I don't trust myself to speak, I might spill all that crap out. So, instead I slowly move closer and wrap my arms around his waist, content to be in his arms for a while.

~*~

Deacon

Leaving Leia at my place was fucking hard, all I wanted to do was keep her in my arms. Feeling her soft curves against me has to be one of best things in the world, apart from her taste that is. But, I had to leave, I need to catch this asshole before any more shit happens. And, I need to talk to Jim, something Leia said had my brain firing on all pistons and I think the lead we have been trying to catch up on since yesterday is starting to make sense. As soon as the words left her mouth, it was like things started lining up in my head.

I'll have to change my locks was all she said. The words play on a loop as I drive to the station. I pull into my spot in the underground carpark and make my way towards the elevator. Rubbing the tension out of the back of my neck, I look up and watch as the numbers light up above the metal doors. I step in when they open and hit the button for my floor. I smile when I picture the look on Leia's face when she first saw my house. A house I never paid much attention to before. Yeah, Jim and I have done a shit load of work to it over the last seven years, but there was never a reason to do it. It just gave us something besides work to concentrate on and using my hands to build something always made me feel good, it reminded me of when my dad and I use to work on my car. It showed me that hard work pays off in the end. But, I've had a feeling deep in my gut since I watched her looking out into the backyard. She was deep in thought and I felt like everything I have done in my life; all the hard work has led me to this moment in time. If Leia is the prize at the end of all this, I will do everything in my power to make sure she is safe and happy. With that thought in mind, and the ding of the elevator doors as they open to my floor, I head straight to my desk. I'm determined to get this shit done and bring this asshole down. Nothing, and I mean nothing, will stop me from giving my woman what she deserves in this life.

"Deacon, what the hell is going on?" Jim stands as I approach him. I'd called him on my way here to explain we needed forensics at Leia's place because someone had broken into her apartment, we needed to dust for prints and anything else this scum could have left behind.

"Did you pull the files of each victim?" I ask, ignoring his question.

"Yeah of course, but we've been over them a million times in the last couple of days"

"We need to run each name through the computer, see if there are any reports about their houses being broken into."

"What are you thinking?" He takes his seat again and opens one of the files sitting on his desk. Reaching over, I grab the next file from the stack, take my seat and flip it open. Moving in front of the computer, I type the victim's name - Lisa Stewart, into the search bar. While the information loads, I take the keys from one of the evidence boxes and pull out the key with the Lisa's name on it. Flipping it in my fingers, I notice the small trademark. I'm guessing it's the company which cut the key. Reaching into a drawer, I remove a magnifying glass and take a closer look. Sure enough, it has an inscription - CLS. Grabbing the other keys, I take a closer look and see each key has the same mark.

"Fuck!"

"What have you got?" Jim asks.

I shake my head wondering again how the hell we missed this. "Each key has the same small inscription, I'm guessing it's from the company which cut the keys." I scrub my face with a hand before locking eyes with Jim. "What the fuck are the chances of them being cut at the same place and not being connected?"

"I don't know, but it's not a coincidence, of that I am fucking sure" He hits something on his computer keyboard. "Bingo!" He swings the screen around to face me and points. I see victim number three's name - Sarah Jacobs, alongside is a report of a break and enter at her residence, two weeks before she was murdered.

I shift focus to my own screen. "Fuck, Lisa Stewart filed a report about two weeks before she was murdered too."

"Let's check the rest of these and see if they have the same, then we can run down the inscription on the keys and try and work out which company cut them."

Nodding, I grab the next file from the pile and get to work. I feel some of the tension from this morning easing, knowing we are one step closer to finding this asshole. I try to push aside all thoughts of the fact; these murders took place two weeks after their residences were broken into. Having a two-week timeline has me on edge and I know Jim has probably come to the same conclusion. I push it to the back of my mind and keep sorting through these files.

Chapter Thirteen

Leia

Deacon brings in my bags and stores them in his walk-in closet, grabs Elvis' leash, brings him into the house and sets up a water bowl for him. He said he'll grab dog food on the way home, the way he says it gives me a thrill, it's like he's telling me it's my home too now. Whoa! I need to slow down, I haven't known the man for a week yet and I'm taking over his life, giving him kids and now claiming his home!

Before he leaves, he kisses me until I'm breathless. The way he kisses me has my legs turning to *Jello* and leaves me breathless. I watch as he leaves, missing him already. I grab my phone and dial Georgie needing to let him know what has happened and where I am before he's blowing up my phone with texts and freaking the fuck out. Sitting on the edge of the bed, I dial his number and listen as it rings, I run fingers over my lips still feeling them tingling.

"Lee Lee."

"Georgie, I just wanted to let you know I'm at Deacon's place. Some shit went down at my place this morning and he brought me here to protect me."

"What's happened?" I hear the worry and panic in his voice.

I try to reassure him I'm fine, but I'm not sure I am. "Someone broke into my apartment."

"Fuck," he grits out and I can just picture him almost passing out.

"Are you okay?" he asks after a moment and I hear the concern in his voice.

"I don't know," I sigh before going on. "I guess, I was at the station with Deacon when it happened."

"Why the hell were you at the police station?"

Ah shit! I probably should have told him about that first. So, I spend the next ten minutes explaining about the tape and how I was taken to the station to make a statement. "Then, when I was finished, Deacon brought me home. We found the door to my apartment had been busted in. He started packing me a bag and said I was staying with him."

"And, there was no room for argument?"

"No, as far as he was concerned it was happening."

"Fuck, Babygirl."

"Tell me about it." I stand and head for the kitchen. I pause mid-step as I'm about to enter the living room. The hairs on my arms stand on end, a shiver gallops down my spine, I feel like I'm being watched. Moving cautiously, I scan the room, but nothing is there. I shake my head, I'm being ridiculous. Heading back to the kitchen, I flip the switch on the kettle. While I wait for the water to boil, I lean against the bench and wonder when I'll get over this feeling of being watched all the time because I refuse to live in fear of my own shadow.

The voice on the tape recording invades my thoughts, clear and frightening. I try to block it out, but it doesn't work and the words play on a loop in my head.

"Do you feel me watching you through the shadows, knowing at any minute I could take you away and nobody will even notice?"

"Leia!" Georgie's shout grabs my attention.

I rub my arm absently and feel goosebumps break out. "Huh? Sorry, I zoned out for a minute." I try to laugh it off, but the ominous feelings of danger are taking control.

"I'll let Michael know what happened, send me the address and we'll come straight there."

"You don't have to, but thank you for offering. I'm going to have a shower and then I'll probably have a nap. Deacon shouldn't be long. I'll be fine." I reassure him, not wanting to ruin any plans they might have made.

"Leia, there was a lot in that sentence that tells me you're not fine. But, if you're sure it's what you want, I won't insist. Ring me if you need anything, even if it's just to talk, okay?"

I nod before realizing he can't see me, so I answer him. "I'm sure, Georgie. I just wanted to let you know where I was. I didn't want you to go to my place, find I wasn't there and worry."

He remains silent for a moment and I suspect he's weighing the truth of my words. He must decide to believe me, he doesn't insist on coming over.

"Okay Babygirl, love ya. Remember, call me if you need anything."

"I promise I will and I love you too."

Disconnecting the call, I place my phone on the bench and bend down to pick up Elvis. I hug him to my chest, thankful nothing had happened to him earlier.

"You're a brave boy." I pat him before kissing the top of his head, he squirms in my arms, trying to lick my face. "What do you say to a nap?" When he barks in response, I take it as a yes and head towards the stairs.

The feeling of being watched engulfs me again and I quickly look around the room – nothing. I shake my head. "Stop it, Leia, you're becoming paranoid."

Straightening my back, I head upstairs. I'll take a nap and not think about what has happened today.

~*~

Deacon

Walking back to the car, after speaking with another locksmith who hadn't cut the keys, I sigh in frustration. I wonder how many more are on the list. I look at Jim, as he rounds the car and opens the driver's side door. When he looks back, I see the same frustration in his face.

"Two more to go." Jim slides behind the wheel.

I nod my head and climb into the car. The time on the dashboard clock catches my eye, it's 4:55pm. The next two places are due to close in five minutes so, we decide to check them out the following morning.

"Let's head back to the station and call it a night, we can start again first thing in the morning." I open my mouth to suggest we take another look at the files, but Jim cuts me off before I get a chance.

"Not sure about you, but my wife wants us to have at least one dinner together this week."

I think about going home to Leia and having dinner, it sounds like a perfect idea. As much as I would have liked to go home with something to tell her, I also want to forget about this shit for a while and hold her in my arms. I felt guilty as shit leaving her alone earlier when she was so scared, but she understood I had a job to do.

I have never met a woman like her before, now I kind of get what my father use to say about my mother. *"Son, the minute I saw your mother I knew in my soul, she was mine. If you ever feel the same way after the first look, hold on and don't let go or you could lose the best thing that ever happens to you. We lose enough in this shitty life without a choice so, when you do get a choice, take it."* I have to admit, I always thought he was full of shit and my parents were just lucky to find each other. But, I have quickly seen the error of my ways and know she is meant to be mine.

"Is Leia staying at your place?" Jim asks.

"Yeah."

"Is that why you have that stupid smile on your face? You look like you could give the Joker a run for his money with that look," he chuckles.

"Shut up, dickhead," I mumble, but I don't care in the slightest that he's laughing at me.

"She's good for you, and you deserve a bit of happiness."

I look over to him and I'm shocked to see the serious look on his face. "When did you become all sappy and shit on me?"

"Caroline!" We both laugh.

"Nah, seriously Black, she seems like a nice girl mixed with sass and it's what you need, someone who can handle your moody ass."

"Well, whether she likes it or not, she ain't never getting away from me now."

"Fuck, was it less than a week ago I was saying you'd be brought to your knees by a woman?"

I don't answer him, I don't want to tell the bastard he's right because I'll never live that shit down. Who would have thought, in less than a week of knowing Leia, she had that effect over me? Shit, who the hell am I trying to kid, the woman brought me to my knees the minute our eyes connected. The night we met, whether we admit it or not, she gave me something I didn't know I was missing. At my silence, Jim starts laughing and mumbles something about wait until I tell Caroline.

~*~

An hour later I pull into the drive of my house, I feel a little excited to get inside and see my woman. Shifting the gears into park, I climb out and lock the car before walking up the path to the front door. As I approach, I hear loud music playing. I chuckle as I let myself in, cross the entryway and head for the living room. I stop dead in my tracks when I reach the doorway and find Leia dancing around the room dressed in her underwear and wearing one of my shirts. My heart thunders against my ribs, I lean against the frame of the door in an effort to find my composure. What I really want to do, is sweep her off her feet and fuck her stupid.

Fuck, she is absolutely stunning, I'm a lucky son of a bitch to be able to call her mine. I listen to the lyrics of the song *Dancing Queen* by *ABBA*. I only know the song because Caroline loves the band.

My attention is drawn back to my woman, I watch as she sways her hips to the beat, her arms wave in the air tightening the shirt over her breasts. I feel myself getting hard, my dick is screaming for release from the confinement of my pants. I can't take much more of this without touching her.

I push off the door frame and approach her slowly so she has a chance to see me and I don't frighten her. She swings around, and the moment she sees me, a huge smile lights up her face. It nearly drops me to my knees. With her eyes closed, she raises her hands into the air, circles her arms and swivels her hips. Fuck, she's sexy. When she attempts to turn around, I gather her to me and slam my mouth down on hers in a bruising kiss. I groan with the sheer ecstasy when I sweep my tongue in to tangle with hers. I feel the moment she lets go, relaxes and lets me take control, it's enough to send me crazy. Tearing my mouth away from hers, I make quick work of the shirt she is wearing before slamming my mouth back to hers. I lift her by the ass and she wraps her legs around my waist as I move to the dining table. Thank fuck nothing is on it, not that it would have mattered, I would have made quick work of clearing it. Laying her down on the tabletop. I pull back and suck, nibble and lick along her neck. She moans as she arches into my touch, her fingers find my hair and when she twists the ends in her fingers, I groan.

"I need you now," I growl. I flip the button on my jeans and pull down the zipper.

"I'm yours," she pants

Fuck, I suck in a breath as her words hit me. Sliding my hands down her body, I reach her underwear and in one quick movement, I rip them from her body. Leaning over, I suck her bottom lip into my mouth and nip lightly as I push two fingers inside her. Curling my fingers upward, I hit her g-spot and rub my palm over her hard clit. She pushes against my hand and I suck down the sexy as fuck sounds coming from her mouth. They are mine and only mine. I pull my fingers from her wet as fuck pussy and bring them to my lips, needing to have her taste while I fuck her. Gripping my cock, I give it a few strokes and rub the pre-cum over the tip before lining myself up at her entrance. I'm about to push in when I remember the condom.

"Fuck, the condom," I growl and start to move, but she wraps her legs around me and holds me in place.

"I'm clean," she pants.

I nod "So am I"

"This is for life." She repeats my words from earlier, moves her hands over her chest, pinches her nipples and the sight about fucking does me in.

"You better fucking believe it." With one hard thrust, I push through her wet folds and push deep within her warm wet heat. My eyes roll back in my head at the sensation of the clench and release of her pussy around me. I grunt, pull back, thrust back in and try not to fucking come.

"Fuck babe, this is not going to last long," I grit out between clenched teeth

"We have all night." She moans as I thrust in and out, while reaching down and rubbing her clit.

"Fuck, Deacon," she whimpers. "Right there, babe."

I look down and watch the rise and fall of her chest, a light sheen of sweat coats her skin and it appears to glow. I can't resist, I lower my head and suck one breast, then the other into my mouth before tracing a line with my tongue up her throat. I suck at her pulse point and the throbbing vibrates through my body. Moving to her mouth, I kiss her hard and hit deep with each thrust. Her body strains towards mine, begging for more.

"Fuck, you feel good," I groan when I pull back from her mouth.

She tightens her muscles around me, I whisper in her ear how good her pussy feels and how wet she is for me. Her body tenses and I know she's close. Thank fuck, for that, I don't know how much longer I can hold on. After two more thrusts, she explodes and takes me over the edge with her.

I rest my forehead against hers, we're both panting hard, gasping for breath. Her fingers run through my hair, her nails graze the back of my neck and my cock hardens again.

"Again?" She giggles and wriggles her bum.

I groan and start to move in and out, slowly this time. "One more time, babe, then we'll eat before we go upstairs for round three."

Her eyes light up and she has a cheeky grin on her face. I bend to kiss her softly before asking, "what is it babe?"

"Can we use your handcuffs next time?"

Fuck me! I swear my cock just got harder. "Anything you want, babe." My mouth hits hers as I thrust harder and deeper, the image of her handcuffed to my bed clear in my mind.

Chapter Fourteen

Leia

After blowing my mind a second time, I stand with Deacon's arms wrapped around me. He chuckles when I sway on shaky legs.

"You right, babe?" His deep voice close by my ear sends a shiver running through me.

"I'm good."

Deacon sniffs the air. "What's that smell?"

"Oh, shit I was cooking a lasagna." I push from his hold and race to the oven hoping it hasn't burned. I grab an oven mitt and open the oven door. The delicious scent, carried on a wave of steam, hits my face. I take the lasagna from the oven and place it on the bench, it's fine.

"It's perfect." I turn and smile at Deacon, when I notice the frown on his face, I don't understand. Then, I look down and notice I'm completely naked and it hits me like a ton of bricks. He's seen my back.

I shift the hot tray onto the chopping board and hurry to find the shirt I was wearing when he arrived home. *Fuck, now I'm saying home!* I grab it from the floor of the living room where it was thrown and slip it on. I keep my back to him, there's no point hiding it now he has seen it, but I don't want to see his face right now. I know I can't put this off any longer, but before I get a chance to explain, his arms wrap around me from behind and I'm instantly cocooned in his warmth. Turning in his arms I place my head against his chest and wrap my arms around his waist.

"Talk to me, babe," he whispers in my ear

"Let me serve up dinner and then I'll explain."

"Okay." He attempts to move away, but I hold him tight, needing a few more minutes.

Heading back to the kitchen, I serve up two plates of food. While I do, I try to figure out how to tell him what happened. There is really no right way to tell him. I sigh deeply, cross to the table and place the plates down. When I start to sit, Deacon drags my chair closer to his.

"Start talking, babe." Deacon forks up a mouthful of food and I can't help staring at the motion, only moments ago that very mouth was devouring my body.

"Babe, I'm waiting."

I shake my head and take a quick sip of the cola Deacon had placed in front of me.

"When I was eighteen I met a boy, I thought he was the love of my life, but a year after we started going out he changed, he became really possessive of me. Abnormally possessive. One night

I was asked to stay late at work, he thought I was cheating on him and when I got home, he was waiting for me. He was so angry, we argued and I started to walk away from him, but he grabbed me by the hair and tried to pull me back. I kicked out and he released me. I managed to make it through the front door and headed for the car to leave. I felt liquid hit me and didn't know what was happening until he lit a match and threw it at me."

Deacon sucks in a noisy breath.

"I was lucky one of my neighbors was out walking her dog at the time. All I remember was trying to rip my shirt off and the searing pain. My lungs felt like they were on fire and then everything went black. I woke up in hospital a couple of days later. I was lying on my stomach and had the worst pain imaginable. I had several skin grafts and many months in hospital. My voice changed from breathing in the superheated air. The top half of my back took the skin grafts better than the lower half. My neighbor, Mrs. Rogers saved my life that night and I'll never be able to thank her enough. After that night, I was wary of men, I wouldn't let anyone close. I didn't trust anyone. I met Georgie at the rehab center and we became really close over time. I knew he was gay and didn't feel threatened, he was the first man I let back in." I take a deep breath, I'm staring at the wall and tears stream over my cheeks. Wiping them away, I hesitate before turning to face Deacon. I'm worried about what I will see in his eyes and when I finally look at him, I note his pissed expression, he's stiff and tense.

I was worried he'd be angry and resolve to pack up my stuff and go to stay with Georgie and Michael. I start to stand and feel the warmth of his touch on my wrist as he wraps his fingers around it.

"It's okay, I understand," I murmur not trusting my voice.

"You understand what?" His voice is husky with emotion.

I don't trust my voice so, I don't say anything at all.

"Babe, I don't know what is going around in that head of yours, but this does not change my opinion of you, if anything it strengthens my feelings." He pauses for a moment, I sit and wait, it seems like he has more he wants to say. "It means my woman is strong as fuck and a fighter."

I feel the tears fall again, but I still don't speak.

Deacon places his fingers under my chin and lifts my head. "Babe, I would never, hear me now - I would *never* hurt you. I only want to be the man you need. Fuck, I want to *deserve* you."

Well damn, here I was wondering if I deserved him and if I was willing to let him in after only knowing him a week. I'm trying to figure out what to say, but I only have one thing I need to say. I grip his hand tight in mine, I know how crazy these feelings are after such a short time, but deep down, everything about this man feels right. I know he would never hurt me, he's proved that over and over again this week. So, I say the two words which are bursting to explode from me.

"For life."

"Fuck yeah, for life, babe." He leans forward and his lips crash against mine in a bruising kiss, leaving me breathless and making my toes curl.

I wish I knew, what I've done in this life to deserve a man like Deacon. He's waltzed into my life, tilted my world on its axis, set my head spinning. If this is what it feels like to be completely accepted, I would do whatever it is over again, to be where I am now.

~*~

Deacon

Leia remains quiet for the rest of dinner and I try to soak in everything she has told me. When she told me what happened to her, I felt an anger so raw, so brutal. But, I'm in absolute awe of her. I can't begin to imagine how she's suffered, what she's been through, to come through even stronger is a fucking miracle. After seeing her back, and hearing her explain what happened, my first thought was to find this fucker and make him pay with his life for what he did to my girl. I know that would end with me in handcuffs and I wouldn't do that to my woman. I hope to Christ she believes I would never hurt her. My attention returns to Leia when she gets to her feet and moves towards the kitchen, yet again I'm captivated by the swing of her hips.

"What you doing, babe?" I drag my eyes away from her ass and look into her eyes when she turns to face me. They're laughing at me, busted! She knows I was staring, I smile. I'm not going to deny it.

"I'm doing the dishes."

I growl and push back from the table, she cooked dinner and she shouldn't have to do the dishes. I can do that. Rounding the kitchen bench, I wrap my arms around her waist and ground my hard cock into her ass. A soft moan escapes her and she pushes her ass back against me. I nip at her shoulder, determined to take her mind off the previous conversation and give her something else to think about.

"Babe, in my world, whoever doesn't cook, washes up. Why don't you go upstairs and have a shower?" She starts to speak, but I shake my head before continuing. "Get your ass up those stairs and have a shower because you, babe, have a date with my handcuffs."

She stands on tiptoes and brushes her lips over mine, her body presses into me and I growl. I can only control myself for so long before I say fuck it and take her up against the sink so, spinning her around, I smack her ass, which causes a yelp and point to the stairs.

"Shower, babe, before I make more of a mess in the kitchen."

"Yes, sir," she giggles and mock salutes.

I can't stop the growl escaping and my very hard cock jumps in my pants at her words. I watch as she heads towards the doorway which leads to the stairs. She stops and pauses for a moment.

"What's up, babe?" I ask as she turns back to me with a strange look on her face.

"Nothing." She shakes her head and heads upstairs.

I turn back to the sink, turning the taps on I get stuck into the dishes. I need to make this quick because the images running through my head of her luscious curves spread out for me, her hands cuffed to the headboard of my bed, has my dick so painful I need to grit my teeth.

~*~

Putting the last dish away, I make my way to the stairs and take them two at a time. I reach the bathroom door, but when I don't hear the sound of running water, I head for the master bedroom. When I enter, she's standing by the window staring out to the backyard. The moonlight wraps around her and she glows. *Fuck, she's gorgeous.* But, I need her ass on the bed. Now!

"Babe, on the bed, now." She swings around on my order and I suck in a deep breath when I finally notice - she's wearing the same Betty Boop underwear and singlet shirt from the first morning I entered her place. "Fuck!" I didn't think it was possible, but my cock just grew thicker and fucking harder.

"Do you like Betty Boop?"

She swings her fucking hips towards me and I know if she touches me, this night will end before it even begins.

"Bed. Now!" I point to the bed. I sound a bit gruffer than I intended but a smile spreads over her face, her eyes shine, and when she licks her lips in anticipation, I groan. When I pull handcuffs from my back pocket, she charges onto the bed, lays down, lifts her hands to grip the headboard and arches her back. *Sexy as fuck.*

Stalking towards her, I lean over the bed and attach one cuff, then the other. Once they click into place, I look into hooded eyes which seem to worship me. That shit hits me in the chest with the force of an out of control truck and I realize, after all she's been through – she totally trusts me. I travel the curves of her body with my eyes and I still can't believe she is all mine.

"Mine," I growl.

"Yes, yours." She sounds breathless, anxious for me.

I lean over and cup her between the legs feeling how wet she is through her underwear. "My pussy." I rotate my palm

"Yours, only ever yours."

Her breathing is more erratic as she becomes more aroused. I stand, I'm dressed only in jeans and they drop to the floor. My eyes are on Leia's, she licks her lips, hunger in her eyes as she watches. My cock leaps forward, curving up to my belly. I stroke my fingers over the length, rubbing pre-cum from the tip with my thumb, I hiss with the need. "You want this?"

She squirms and nods her head.

Fuck, I need her mouth. Crawling up from the bottom of the bed, I kiss, nip and suck at her slowly until I'm resting above her chest, my cock hovering above her mouth. As I lock eyes with her, I tease her lips. Her eyes are pleading with me to give her what she wants.

"I want your mouth," I grit out.

I watch as her tongue darts out, she licks the tip causing me to hiss in pleasure. She opens her mouth wide, I close my eyes when I feel the wet warmness surround my hard cock. Opening my eyes after a few seconds, I lean forward and grip the headboard, needing support as her mouth sucks and licks. I drop my head on a groan when she moans around my cock and the vibration travels through me.

"Fuck, babe."

I pull out and she whimpers at the loss. I slide down and kiss her hard, tasting a little of myself on her.

"I need you," she pants out when I break the kiss.

Running my hands down her body, I slide down until my face is lined up with her pussy. I pull her undies down her smooth legs and throw them to the floor. Leaning forward, I slide my hands under her ass and lift, burying my face in her wetness, licking and sucking until she's bucking into me. Sexy moans leave her mouth. I latch onto her clit and suck hard while I grip her hips tighter, she has no place to go, she has to take everything I'm doing to her. I feel her legs tense and as much as I want to suck up her orgasm, I want to feel it wrapped around my cock. Placing her back on the bed, she says something I don't quite understand, but before she has a chance to say anything else, I slam into her. She screams as her body locks up with her release and I grit my teeth as I hold myself back from coming.

"Fucken Heaven," I growl out as I thrust in and out as hard and as deep as I can. The clenching of her pussy muscle has me feeling pure fucking ecstasy like the first time I laid eyes on her.

"Mine. Forever mine." I can't seem to stop telling her, I need her to understand.

"Yours. Forever yours." She wraps her legs tighter around me and arches her body harder into mine.

"Fuck, babe." I grab the bottom of her singlet shirt, slide it up and wrap it around her hands with the cuffs. Then I run my hand down until I'm cupping her breast, I give her nipple a light twist and feel her body tense at the movement.

"Fuck babe, you like that." I thrust in, twist her nipple again which causes a loud moan to fill the room.

She pushes back taking me deeper.

"Ah shit, babe." I'm not sure how much longer I can last.

"Right there, Deacon. Don't stop."

"Never." I thrust in one more time and feel her exploding all over my cock, I can't hold back this time.

I let go and grunt out her name at the same time she screams mine. It soothes my fucking soul hearing her voice screaming my name in absolute fucking pleasure. Taking a moment to get our breaths back, I reach over, grab the key, release the cuffs and untangle her shirt. I then massage her wrists before pulling her into my chest, I hear her sighs. Wrapping my arms around her tighter, I feel her relax. I marvel at how good it feels to have her softness against my hardness, I close my eyes and picture doing this every night for the rest of our lives.

~*~

I jolt awake at a high-pitched scream and instantly I'm on alert. Reaching for my gun, I flip on the lamp. I look around, but don't see anything. Leia is sitting up, breathing hard, tears streaming from her eyes. I reach forward and pull her into my arms.

"What is it, babe?"

Breathing heavily, she takes a moment before answering.

"Shadows, darkness," she babbles into my chest. When she pulls back, I note her wild eyes and the stark fear within.

"Don't let the shadow take me," she pleads.

Fuck, she has obviously had a nightmare about the tape she listened to earlier. I pull her closer and reassure her, I would never let anything happen to my girl. I listened to the tape when she was in the interview with Jim and can understand why she's having nightmares. The recording was scratchy as fuck and it's done that way so the victim will fear them. Fuck, I should have spoken to her about this earlier, but so much had happened and when I got back home, I couldn't wait to have her in my arms.

"Babe, rest now." I kiss the top of her head as her breathing starts to calm. "I will never let anything happen to you." I rub my hand up and down her back hoping to soothe her. And, for what seems like the ten millionth time in the last couple of days, I swear I will find this piece of shit and make him pay.

Chapter Fifteen

Leia

I awoke this morning with Deacon's head between my legs, his tongue caused my body to melt and screams bounced off the walls. It certainly diverted my thoughts from the nightmare I'd had earlier. Sitting alone in his living room, I set up the laptop to get some work done, but it's so quiet, I can't quite concentrate. I reach down and pat Elvis's head while he snoozes soundlessly in my lap. Flashbacks of the nightmare run rampant through my head causing me to feel helpless all over again.

I was lost in the darkness, and cold, so cold my breath floated white on the otherwise still air. I wandered aimlessly, trapped in what seemed like an endless tunnel. Running, trying to find any trace of light, sliver of hope. Stopping, I looked towards some kind of cave, a light off in the distance and then darkness. But, I could hear noises which sent chills down my spine. Venturing forward, I run my hand over the wall to help guide my way. I refused to look back, worried at what I might see. A door handle! I open the door and enter a dimly lit room. Georgie and Michael were there laughing and for the first time, I feel relief wash over me. I'm safe. Then fear, I want to run to them, but I can't move, it's like I'm anchored in concrete. George and Michael's laughter turns to screaming and I watch in horror as they melt into puddles before me. Deacon, he's here, big and strong. Why couldn't I move? We reached for each other, but it was like a force was pushing us apart. I was screaming at him to help me. Then, a shadow of a man came up behind Deacon, chills cause my body to shake, tears poured from my eyes as he pulled a gun and fired. Deacon was on the floor in a puddle of blood, I screamed and reached for him, begging for help, pleading with the shadow to leave us alone, but he wouldn't listen. Then, Shadow spoke, and the scratchy voice echoed around me.

"I told you I would come from the shadows and nobody can stop me from taking what I want."

I don't remember much after that. Deacon's arms had wrapped around me, he pulled me close to his chest and his soft voice whispered in my ear that he had me now and he would never let anything happen to me.

But, you know the feeling you get after watching a really scary movie, how you hear sounds that aren't there, or you think you see something moving through the night? It's the feeling I've had since I woke last night and it's running through me right now. Pushing to my feet, I need to clear my head and find the strength I have fought so long for. I cross to Deacon's stereo, find the dock for my iPod and push play on a song. I don't really care what it is, I just need something to break me out of this funk and get rid of this silence.

Elvis barks and dances around my feet as the beat thumps and the words ring out. God, I love *ACDC* and I love this song - *You Shook Me All Night Long*. I let the music take over my body and lose myself in song after song until I'm feeling a little better. A loud banging at the door startles me, I lower the volume of the music and take a few deep breaths as I make my way to the door with Elvis on my heels. Reaching the door, I lean forward and peer through the peephole. I'm not sure why, it's not like I know anyone around here. It could be the bloody postman for all I know, I still wouldn't have a clue who he was. Standing on tiptoe, I hold an eye to the hole and smile when I see Georgie and Mickey standing outside. I fling open the door and the men smile back at me, they have bags in their hands.

"How did you find out Deacon's address?" They point behind them and Mickey steps to the side, Caroline is standing there smiling.

"I let you have last night, but today you will spill the beans. Oh, and we want to hear *all* the juicy details of your night with that man hunk of yours." Georgie and Mickey push past me as I laugh.

"Leia honey, Deacon is like a son to me, so maybe leave out some of the details." Caroline laughs as she wraps her arm around my waist, guides me inside and kicks the door closed with her foot. We head through to the living room as I laugh with her. Fuck, it feels good to laugh and smile. I knew Georgie wouldn't believe me last night when I said I was fine, I'm glad he knows me so well.

~*~

Turns out the bags the boys were holding, were full of food from my favorite Italian restaurant. God, I think I love the boys even more now. Caroline pulls out plates and the boys open containers on the kitchen bench. I inhale the yummy smell and my stomach growls in response. When I check the clock, which hangs on the wall above the kitchen bench, I notice it's just after one in the afternoon. No wonder I'm hungry, I must have been lost in thought for longer than I realized. After stacking food onto our plates, we move to the dining table and take a seat, Mickey grabs everyone a drink. Taking my first mouthful, I moan around the fork as flavors assault my taste buds, the others laugh at me.

"I'm not even sorry," I sigh and scoop up another forkful. "It's so good."

"Okay Babygirl, spill your guts," Georgie says as he tastes a mouthful of food.

I groan, place my fork down on the table and run my hands down my face knocking my glasses off my nose. I settle them back in place and tell the others everything that happened yesterday. When I finish speaking, I glance around the table and wait for them to say something.

Caroline is the first to break the silence. "Oh God, sweetie." She places her hand over her chest. I nod.

"So, Deacon and Jim are all over this?" Mickey asks.

I nod again and turn towards Georgie, he's yet to speak, I know he's trying to process what he's heard.

"So, some sick, twisted piece of shit left you a tape on your doormat and when you finally remembered it, you give it to Deacon."

I start to speak but Georgie holds up a finger and I snap my mouth shut.

"To continue, you hand the tape over, *after* you listen to it. Then, Deacon escorts you home, where you find someone has broken in so, he brings you here to keep you safe."

I nod, wondering where he is going with this.

"Last night you rang me and explained some of this. And, you wonder why we're here today?"

"You knew last night?" Mickey asks Georgie.

"Yeah, but she didn't tell me everything so, I didn't mention it until we saw Leia and got the facts." Georgie explains to Mickey who nods his understanding.

"How are you feeling?" Georgie places his hand over mine.

"Scared shitless," I answer honestly. I'm not feeling hungry anymore so, I push my plate away.

"Try to eat something Lee Lee." Mickey pushes the plate back in front of me.

"Okay, let's dig in before this yummy food gets cold. We can talk more about this when we're finished." Caroline gives me a soft smile.

~*~

Deacon

Jim parks the car in front of the last locksmith on our list. This has to be the one, otherwise I don't know what the hell to do, this is the only lead we have. I don't need it to run cold right now, we have got to hit on something soon.

Jim steps up beside me and nods towards the doors. I stride up the path, noticing the large sign hanging above the door and a sticker fixed to the glass door, they read - Col's LockSmiths. I note the capital *CLS* on the sign and sticker are a similar style to those on the keys. My hopes rise. When I push through the door, a chime above sounds. I glance over my shoulder to Jim I can see by the look he gives me, he's noted the sign too. I approach the counter and a young blonde woman, probably in her late twenty's, comes from the back room and steps up to the glass counter.

"Hello gentlemen, how can I help you today?" I don't miss the way her eyes check me out.

Sorry sweetheart I'm happily taken by a beautiful dark haired beauty with eyes the color of wine I could easily get drunk from. Jim nudges me and I shift the focus from thoughts of my woman and get my head back in the game.

"This is my partner Detective Deacon Black and I'm Detective Jim Barnes." Jim flashes his badge and I show her mine before sliding it back onto my belt. I scan the room noting the wall of keys behind the woman. Jim takes the lead after the woman introduces herself.

"My name is Charlotte Wallace."

"We need to speak to the owner, Colin Wallace."

She gives Jim a sad look. "I'm sorry, but he isn't available anymore."

"I'm sorry, Miss Wallace." Jim picks up on the sadness in her voice as well.

"It's fine, I run things now. What can I do for you today?"

"We'd like to look at some keys and see if you recognize them. We're investigating a series of murders in the area and the keys were found with the last victim." Jim pulls out the evidence bag and places it on the glass counter.

I watch closely as she looks down and see her eyes widen and nose flare. I would have missed it if I wasn't watching her reaction so closely.

"You recognize them?" I'm not going to play games.

She's silent for a moment, seemingly weighing her words. Irritation crawls through me as the silence lingers. I don't have the time, or the patience, to wait any longer.

"We can arrest you for obstruction," I grit out trying to hold onto my failing control.

"No, wait. They have been cut by us, but they don't come from here."

"What do you mean they don't come from here? They have your trademark stamped on them and they're the same brand as the keys hanging on the wall behind you." I'm about done with this bullshit.

"Yeah, they do, but we have a mobile service. These have been cut on the road. See this circle here…." She holds a key out to us and we see a tiny circle alongside the trademark. I assumed it was part of the mark. "….only keys cut on the road have this circle, that's how I know they aren't from here. The guy on the road has his own set of keys so we can tell them apart from the shop cut keys. They go to people's homes and cut on site.

"We need a list if everyone who has cut mobile keys for the past five years," Jim demands.

"Um," she pauses again

"Miss Wallace, we can take this down to the station if we need to," Jim says with a hard edge to his voice, he's getting sick of her games too. He may be putty for his wife and likes to joke around, but when he's working a case, he's a hard man you don't want to piss off.

"Only my brother does the mobile keys while I run the shop, since our father passed away last year, my brother wouldn't do this."

"We need your brother's name, Miss Wallace." She stares at Jim when he speaks, glances at me and then her shoulders slump in defeat, she knows we'll find out with or without her help. "Pete Wallace." She scrubs her face with her hands.

"We need a contact number." Jim pulls out his notepad.

I roll the name around in my head, something clicks and I stiffen when I realize how I know the name. "Son of a bitch," I snarl.

Jim looks at me as Charlotte turns to grab her phone.

"What?" Jim asks quietly so only I can hear him.

"We had the son of a bitch!" I drag fingers through my hair. "It's Donald's fucking drug dealer!"

"Fucken hell," Jim mumbles. I watch as things start clicking into place in his mind before the sound of bullets ring out.

~*~

What the fuck? Diving for cover, I try to look through the shattered glass doors hoping to see who is firing. I pull out my gun and take aim. I look around for Jim to make sure he's good, I see him on the ground, not moving and blood is pooling around him.

"Fuck!! Fuck!!" I crawl to where he is.

The gunshots stop and I hear the squeal of tires. When I look back toward the doors, I note the glass has now broken away and I see the ass end of a white van with *CLS* on the back panel. *Fucken Pete!* Returning my focus to Jim, I press down on the wound in his chest causing him to groan. I grab the radio from my belt and call it in - *Officer Down!*

"Jim!" I shout trying to rouse him. "Fuck Jim, wake the fuck up!" I watch as his eyes flicker open. He stares straight at me but doesn't speak.

"Fuck partner, don't do that, keep your eyes on me, okay?" I nod and he opens his mouth to speak.

"Does that mean we're going steady?" he wheezes out and groans as I push a bit harder.

"Fuck Jim," I chuckle. Even fucking shot he wants to bust my balls. "Your wife will kill me if you die."

He grabs my hand and I watch as his eyes start to close again. "You tell her and my boy I love them."

"You can fucking tell them yourself when we get your ass to the hospital." I hear the sounds of sirens in the distance and look around to see if Charlotte was hurt, but she's nowhere to be seen.

"Deacon," Jim says pulling my attention back to him.

"You got this partner, the ambulance is close, keep your eyes on me and stop trying to be fucking funny." I feel myself break out in a cold sweat at the thought of him dying and I know I can't lose him, I *will not* lose him.

A few moments later, the place is a flurry of activity. I'm pushed aside as the EMT's take over. I scoot back on my ass to give them room to work and watch as they attach an oxygen mask to his face and push gauze onto the wound. The bleeding doesn't stop, they pack more gauze into place and hold it firm while he's lifted onto a gurney. They hurry toward the waiting ambulance and lift him in.

My breathing is rapid as I look down at my hands, they're covered in blood, Jim's blood and I'm shaking. Fuck, he can't die. Ever since I lost my parents, he's been there for me. I shake the thought from my head, the man is strong as fuck and I know he won't give up. I pull out my phone, I don't want to make this call but I don't have a choice. Pressing speed dial, I lift it to my ear and listen as it rings a few times before she picks up.

"Caroline, it's Jim……"

Chapter Sixteen

Leia

After lunch, we clean up and I excuse myself to run upstairs to put some clothes on, I'm dressed only in tiny sleep shorts and one of Deacon's shirts. I know none of them care about what I'm wearing, but Georgie suggested we slip out to the shops and grab stuff for dinner. Tiny shorts and a shirt just wouldn't do.

Underwear, black sundress, black sandals and hair in a ponytail, I'm ready. I head downstairs, running my hand over the beautifully carved banister, the detail is exquisite. The boys are playing around with my iPod and I hear *Runaround Sue* by *Dion* playing. I skip the rest of the way down the stairs and head for the living room. Caroline jumps to her feet and starts to sing and dance to the beat, I grab her hand and we laugh. We're twisting and shaking our stuff as we dance around the coffee table and the boys laugh at our display. For the first time today, I start to feel my old self again. It's amazing how listening to good music and having my friends around can perk up my attitude. I know a lot of things are up in the air at the moment and stuff is happening that I don't understand, but at this moment, I try not to let it affect me. I shift my focus to something I can control. One song morphs into another and we're breathless by the time I head to the fridge to grab us all drinks.

Caroline's phone rings and she laughs as she answers the phone. "Where?" Caroline whispers and I hear the crack in her voice.

The air seems to be sucked out of the room and ice runs through my veins. I turn to the boys and see the grim expressions on their faces as they stand watching Caroline. Fuck, what's happened, is Deacon okay? My stomach twists at the thought something has happened to him. What if something has happened to Jim? Oh God no, I just met these beautiful people, I can't lose any of them.

I watch as Caroline nods and tears slide down her cheeks. She is struggling to speak so Georgie gently takes the phone from her.

I move to gather her into my arms while Georgie speaks into the phone. "It's George, Caroline is too upset to speak."

Silence.

"Oh, Deacon, what's going on?"

Relief floods me knowing Deacon is okay but then fear grips me, knowing it must be Jim. I hold Caroline closer and guide her into a chair.

"Shit, okay, we'll bring the girls straight there." Georgie disconnects the call and squats in front of us, he squeezes

Caroline's hand. "Mickey and I are going to take you to the hospital."

Caroline nods and Georgie helps her to her feet. I stand and wrap my arm around her, guiding her towards the front door. She's become very quiet, I think she's in shock.

~*~

Georgie pulls up to the hospital doors and Caroline and I jump from the car, leaving the boys to park the car. The shock seems to have worn off and she is both pissed and worried about the man she loves dearly. For one second, I almost feel sorry for whoever has harmed him because if she finds him first, I know she won't hesitate to kill the son of bitch.

Georgie explained what little he knew on the way to the hospital. We know Jim was shot and Deacon said he'll do his best to find out whatever he could before we arrived at the hospital. The glass sliding doors whoosh apart and we head straight for the information desk. Deacon's voice echoes down the hall from where we are standing and I can tell by his tone he's pissed, but I also hear the worry in his voice. My heart breaks for him and tears roll over my cheeks as we head straight towards him. He's standing talking to a man in a white coat and despite my anxious state of mind, I can't help but notice how his muscles flex as he waves his arms in the air. He's annoyed and I know my man is in full swing right now, one wrong word from the Doctor will have him going over the edge.

"Doc you better start talking English instead of that medical mumbo jumbo or you and I are not going to be friends. If I don't get answers soon…"

"Deacon!" Caroline says with an edge to her voice.

Deacon stops speaking mid-sentence and swings around to see us approaching him. When I look towards the Doctor, I see relief wash over his face. I ignore the fact my man was scaring the shit out of him and lock eyes with Deacon. My heart breaks a little more at the sight of worry and fear in his eyes.

Caroline steps into his outstretched arms, he hugs her and whispers something in her ear. She nods into his chest while he stares straight at me.

"Excuse me." Caroline straightens and steps out of Deacon's hold. She stomps up to the Doctor, hmmm, if it was fear in his eyes when Deacon was dealing with him, right now he looks like he might piss himself.

Caroline points a beautifully manicured nail at the Doctor, but doesn't touch him. "Now! You listen here, Doc, and listen good. If you don't give me answers about my husband right now and in words I can understand, then what detective Black wants to do to you has nothing on what I will do. Capisce? Answers, now!"

I watch as the doctor swallows hard and flips open the file in his hands. He explains what's happening with Jim in language a teenager could understand, yep, he got the message. While we listen to Caroline and the Doc, deep in conversation, Deacon pulls me into his arms. I melt against him and soak in his familiar intoxicating aftershave.

"Babe," Deacon whispers in my ear.

I look up at him and he wipes the tears from my eyes.

"Please tell me Jim will be okay."

Deacon shakes his head. "The Doc said it's touch and go at the moment. But, he's strong as fuck and I told him, he has no option, he is going to pull through." He rubs his hand up and down my back and I know he's trying to reassure himself as well as me. I feel like shit, he's focusing on trying to reassure me when his partner and best friend is fighting for his life.

"Georgie and Mickey will have parked the car by now. I'll go and get them and grab us a drink while you stay here with Caroline."

Deacon holds me closer, not willing to let me go.

I nod towards Caroline who is still talking to the doctor and signing some forms. "Caroline needs you right now and I'll only be five minutes."

Reluctantly he loosens his hold, bends down and kisses my lips softly. I head down the corridor towards the front doors and look back over my shoulder, Deacon wraps his arm around Caroline's shoulders and listens to the doctor. *Fuck, Jim needs to be okay.*

~*~

Deacon

I watch as Leia turns and heads towards the front doors, I can't seem to take my eyes off her ass as it sways, it's fucking hypnotic. I wrap my arm around Caroline's shoulder and pull her closer to me. I'm trying hard to concentrate on what the Doctor is saying, but in all honesty, the moment the girls turned up and I saw Caroline's face, it almost broke me and everything went to shit.

I glance around and notice a male orderly staring at my girl's ass as she leaves, a growl escapes and my muscles tense. I want to smash his face into the nearest door for staring at my woman. He looks over and notices me scowling at him, his head jerks away and his eyes drop to the floor, something down there became very interesting all of a sudden. It's clear from his actions, he understands, she's mine.

Caroline slaps my chest, bringing my focus back to the conversation and I look down to see a small smile touch her lips. "Deacon, be a caveman later," she says before returning to the conversation with the doctor. Fuck, I need to get my shit together and concentrate on what is going on with Jim.

"When can I see him?" Caroline asks.

"He's having emergency surgery to remove the bullet and then he'll be moved to ICU for forty-eight hours. He'll be monitored closely and once his vitals are stabilized, he'll be moved to a private room." The doctor's response helps settle my nerves, but I know anything could happen between now and then.

I draw Caroline closer when I feel her body trembling against me. As much as she's putting on a brave face right now, I know she's an absolute wreck on the inside. The doctor strides off to where I assume the theatre suites are and a thought hits me.

"Doc," I call out, he turns to face me. "As soon as the bullet is removed we need it to go straight to forensics."

"I'll have it sent out to you as soon as it's out."

"Thanks, Doc."

He turns and pushes through a door marked *Staff Only*.

"What are you thinking?" Caroline steps back from my hold and stares up at me, as much as I don't want to tell her the details of what happened, I can let her know what is bothering me.

"You know Jim and I wear bulletproof vests when we're on the job?"

Caroline looks at me hard for a minute before nodding. I watch as the expression on her face changes when she realizes what I'm thinking. "Armor piercing bullets, fuck!"

I nod. Caroline is as quick as a whip and I knew she would get where I was going.

~*~

"Black!" The Lieutenant's voice booms from somewhere down the hall and I turn to see him approaching. Fast.

"Fuck," I grit out.

"Mrs. Barnes." The Lieutenant nods at Caroline as he comes to a stop in front of us.

"Lieutenant Stevenson," Caroline smiles.

"Don't worry ma'am, we'll get this son of bitch," he assures her.

Caroline nods before heading to the room where the Doctor asked us to wait.

The Lieutenant turns his attention to me. "Black, you're off the case."

Fuck, I knew this was coming, but before I can answer, he continues.

"You should have been pulled a few days ago, you're too close to this."

"How?" I challenge, not thinking he knows about Leia. But, I'm a fucking idiot if I think he doesn't know shit.

"Black, do not test my patience right now. You can't possibly be thinking clearly. Barnes has been shot, and if that's not enough to piss you off and make you go for blood with this asshole, Miss James is your girl and heavily involved, am I right?" He raises a challenging eyebrow at me.

I don't usually take kindly to being challenged, despite him being my boss, but I know if I push, he'll take my badge. I simply nod my head.

"I'm not a fucken idiot, I left it alone because Barnes interviewed your girl, but now this piece of shit is making it personal and I don't need you going off halfcocked in an attempt to get this asshole. So, keep your ass here with Mrs. Barnes or take your ass home. I don't give a fuck which one you choose, but as of right now, you're on leave. You keep your ass out of this, do you understand me?"

"I have other cases I can work, sir."

"Give me some credit, if I let you into the station to work, you'll poke your nose into this case. You have your choices, here or home. Am. I. Clear?"

Fuck! "Yes sir," I snarl between clenched teeth. I'm not at all fucking pleased, but I understand I have put him between a rock and a hard place. He has superiors to answer to and if he doesn't keep me in line, we could both lose our badges. So, I say nothing more about it, but I need to know who the fuck will be taking over the case. Regardless of who it is, *I* will be looking out for my girl.

"Who will be taking over the case?"

"I'm going to kick it back to Jacobs and Ryan."

The words have barely left his mouth when I look over the lieutenant's shoulder and see them both striding towards us. At the same time Leia hurries up the hallway carrying drinks. I watch as Jacob checks out my girl. *Fuck, is it going to be a constant battle with other men every time she's in public? Maybe I should handcuff her to my bed permanently so, I don't kill every motherfucker who checks out my girl. Fuck now that would be something to come home to every nigh*t. Leia steps up and drapes her free arm over mine, I wrap my arm around her and pull her close to my side. I narrow my eyes at the pricks standing in front of me, yeah, they hear my warning, loud and clear. Lieutenant Stevenson introduces himself and she lets go of me to shake his hand.

"It's nice to meet you, Lieutenant."

"Nice to meet you too, Miss James."

"Babe, why don't you take the drinks to Caroline in the waiting room?" I point to the open room a little further up the hallway.

She stands on tiptoe and kisses my cheek before nodding to the other men. I watch as she goes before turning back to Jacobs and telling him how it is. Yeah, I turned caveman.

"If you want to keep your sight, I'd advise you not to check out my woman again, Jacobs."

Stevenson chuckles and slaps me on my back before heading towards the waiting room. I'm left alone with Jacobs and Ryan and I see the shadow of understanding cross Jacob's eyes when he realizes what I'd said.

He smiles as he speaks. "Noted man, but we'll need to talk to her at some stage."

"Not without me. I may be off this case but there's no fucking way you're talking with her alone." I spin on my heels and head towards the waiting room, not giving a fuck if they have an issue with my words or not. No way in fucking hell are they talking to my woman without me there.

~*~

I enter the waiting area and observe Stevenson on his phone. My girl is sitting beside Caroline and I watch as she passes her a drink before wrapping an arm around her shoulder. Taking a seat next to my girl, I drape my arm across the back of her seat. A few moments later, Jacobs and Ryan walk in followed by Georgie and Mickey. I lift my chin in greeting to Leia's friends before they take seats on the other side of Caroline.

I settle deep into thought and wonder if I could have done more at the scene to protect and help Jim. I just don't know what else I could have done differently. I breath out hard, Leia lays her hand on my thigh and gives it a reassuring squeeze. I soak in her touch and try to calm my ass down; this waiting is driving me crazy and has me on edge. I know I won't be able to relax until the doctor walks in and tells me Jim is out of danger. I concentrate on Leia's fingers as she absently draws small circles on my thigh, she must feel me relax a little as she squeezes my leg again. Fuck, Mathew!

"Caroline, do you want me to go and grab Mathew from school?"

She shakes her head and Georgie explains. "She rang the school from the car on the way here, she told them she had an emergency and I'll be picking him up." Georgie places a hand over Caroline's. "She didn't want him to worry."

I nod, settle back in my chair and tilt my head back to rest against the wall. I close my eyes, but open them again when the scene insists on replaying on a loop in my head. I wrap my hand around the back of Leia's neck and play with the strands of hair at the nape of her neck. I'm trying to take my mind off everything, I feel her shiver. *Hmmm, interesting.* I love how her body comes alive with just one touch, images of her laid out for me last night jump to mind and I shake my head clear. My cock is now as hard as fucking steel. I must have a pained look on my face because Leia leans over and kisses my cheek. She speaks softly.

"Babe, Jim is going to be fine."

I nod, it's killing me not knowing what is happening with Jim, but I can't help wanting to feel Leia beneath me. Now! *Fuck, get your shit together! Get your priorities right,* I chastise myself for about the tenth time today.

Chapter Seventeen

Leia

After more hours than I can count, a doctor walks in with a grave look on his face and tired eyes. I grip Deacon's leg, my nails dig into his thigh, it tenses beneath my fingers.

Caroline and Mathew stand and wait impatiently for word on Jim's condition.

The Doctor steps closer. "Mrs. Barnes, your husband is being moved to ICU as we speak. He suffered severe blood loss and Code Blue was called twice while he was on the table."

"Code Blue?" Mathew asks as he wraps his arms around his mother.

Deacon stands to be with them.

The Doctor directs his words to Mathew. "Code Blue is a Cardiac Arrest – Heart Attack..."

"My dad had two heart attacks?"

"He did, but we got him back and stabilized him." He returned his attention to Caroline. "Mr. Barnes has been put into a medically induced coma and has a ventilator breathing for him to allow his body to rest and recover."

"Will dad be okay?" Mathew's voice is teary.

The Doctor, to his credit, speaks honestly. "We're doing all we can to make sure your dad comes through this. He doesn't look good at the moment with all the machines hooked up, but he's fighting."

Mathew nods

"Can I see him," Caroline asks in a soft voice.

"In about an hour, I'll send a nurse to come and get you. We have to make sure the medications and machines are doing their jobs and there won't be another emergency."

"Thank you, Doctor."

"We're taking good care of your husband, Mrs. Barnes," the Doctor assures her before leaving.

Caroline drops into a chair, hugging her son as tears roll over her cheeks. Deacon wraps his arms around them and whispers words in Caroline's ear.

I look towards Georgie and Mickey and see this has affected them too. Even though these people haven't been in our lives for very long, it hurts because we have become really close. I send an express prayer to God asking that Jim makes it out alive, there is too much love for this man for him to leave us now.

~*~

An hour later the nurse enters and tells Caroline, Jim is stable and they can see him. There is a maximum of three visitors at any one time. Deacon stands with Caroline and Matthew, but looks towards me before going with them. I nod, I know how badly he wants to see his partner.

"Are you sure, babe?"

"Don't be silly, of course I'm sure. Go and make sure your partner is okay."

He crosses the room to me, bends and kisses me softly before straightening and hurrying through the door.

"Lee Lee, come on, we'll grab some coffee while they visit with Jim." Georgie holds out his hand.

I welcome the chance to get to my feet and stretch after sitting in an uncomfortable plastic chair for hours. My body aches and as soon as I know Jim is okay, I want to crawl into bed with Deacon in my arms, grateful he's okay.

~*~

When we return to the waiting room with our fresh hot coffees, we find a woman roughly my age with blonde hair standing near the door. She has a bandage wrapped around the top of her arm and she looks lost.

"Are you okay," I ask as we make our way over to her.

She gives me a strange look before she shakes it away and clears her throat. "Um yeah, I heard one of the detectives who was in my shop today was shot, I wanted to make sure he was okay?"

"Oh, um..." I bite my lip. I'm wondering how much to tell this stranger when Georgie cuts in.

"We're not sure at the moment."

A look flashes across her face. I can't quite read what it is, but it's gone as quick as it came. When she next looks at me she is sizing me up. "That's okay, I'll contact Deacon later and find out what's going on."

The way she speaks Deacon's name gets my back up and sets me on alert. It's as if they know each other on an intimate level. I study her carefully, really take her in. She's quite pretty actually, with blonde hair and blue eyes and a slim figure that seems to go on for miles. Much nicer than my curvy shape. A thought crosses my mind - Deacon and I have never discussed if he was mine alone like I was only his. Fuck, what if he's sleeping with her too? I feel violently ill!

"No worries," Georgie says to her as she leaves and leads me into the waiting room. He turns me to face him. "Lee Lee, stop it. Get that thought out of your mind. I'm sure there is nothing going on between them."

I would have believed him if he hadn't had just confirmed, I didn't imagine the seductive way she said his name.

"Babygirl, he only has eyes for you," Mickey assures me.

I can't stop thinking about his hands touching her or her experiencing his kisses I love so much. I can't control the anger swelling within me, I have to get out of this room, away from this hospital. I need to go somewhere to think. The rational side of my brain is telling me to speak to Deacon before jumping to conclusions, but right now there is so much going on, I just need to be alone and breathe.

"Mickey, can you take me back to Deacon's place?"

"Don't think about doing anything stupid before you speak to Deacon, Leia," Georgie warns.

He knows me too fucking well and it pisses me off with how he knows what I'm thinking. "I won't, I just need to lay down, I'm bloody exhausted. You wait here then you can give me a call and let me know how Jim is doing. There's no point in me staying, Deacon probably won't leave and I won't be able to see Jim until tomorrow."

Georgie nods, leans over and says something to Michael before kissing him goodbye. I turn away at the show of affection and my eyes well with tears. I need to lay down, I need sleep. I've had more than enough for one day. Grabbing my bag, I slip it onto my shoulder and head for the door. I contemplate whether or not I should send Deacon a message, but don't bother. He won't get it anyway, they can't have their phones on where they are.

Stepping out into the night, I take a few deep breaths of the cool night air and watch as Mickey heads to get the car. I debate what I'll do. Go to Deacon's place, pack up my things, grab Elvis and head back to my place. Or, go to Deacon's, have a shower, get some sleep and talk to him like an adult in the morning.

Fuck, I pull up my big girl panties knowing I have to go with option two. I need to know where I stand, I'm not going to jump to conclusions and run away. Mickey pulls to a stop in front of me and I climb into the car. I know I'm doing the right thing, I'm exhausted after hardly any sleep last night and with everything that's happened today, I need to rein my crazy ass in before I unload on Deacon. I don't think he needs my needy ass whining at him right now with everything that's going with Jim and the case.

~*~

Deacon

I step out into the cool night air, anxious to get home. My muscles are tense and anger slices through me at the thought my girl would think I'm seeing someone behind her back. As soon as I returned to the waiting room and saw she was gone, my anxiety spiked.

George explained what had happened with Charlotte, I don't understand her game. Why would she try to make Leia think I had anything with her for fucks sake? I only met her today, but then, I told Leia, the moment I looked at her I knew she was the one for me. Maybe she thinks I look at every woman like that.

I rake my nails through my hair in frustration as we head towards George's car, I feel an overwhelming need to get to Leia. If she's not at my place when I get there, I'll go to her apartment and drag her ass back to mine kicking and screaming if I have to. I'll force her to listen to me, understand she's the one. The only. As for Charlotte, I'll deal with the bitch later and she better be able to tell me where her brother is. Just because Stevenson took me off the case, doesn't mean I won't chase up a few leads on my own. Especially when some bitch, who I know must have told her brother we were on to him, wants to mess with my woman's head. I need to go back to the station for my car, but I don't want to take the time right now. I've asked George to take me home.

"Can you grab me in the morning so I can get my car from the station?"

"Yeah, no probs." He nods and gives me a strange look, I can see he wants to say something else.

"Just spit it out, it's been a long fucking day."

"Leia, is like a sister to Mickey and me, I need to know you don't plan on screwing her over. She's dealt with more than enough in her life and doesn't need you playing games with her."

Anger slices through me again, but I try to calm down. I know this man means the world to Leia and I don't want to cause more shit between her and I because I let loose on her best friend. Also, I can't be angry at him for looking out for her.

"I'm going to say this once, and only once, so listen closely. Leia means the world to me…." George starts to interrupt, but I hold up my hand. "I know you're thinking I have only known her for a week, but trust me when I say, she is it for me. The minute my eyes locked on her, I was gone. One look. One. Fucking. Look. And, I knew I had to make her mine. I would lay my whole goddamn world at her feet if that's what she wants, or needs, to understand she is mine and I'm hers. Nothing, and I mean *nothing*, will get in the way of me making her mine in every way. I will marry that girl." I breath out hard and realize how irritated I am. "Does that answer your question?" I sound calmer than I feel.

He stays silent for a moment and I wonder what the hell he is thinking. Then he laughs! What the fuck, laughing?

"What's so fucking funny?" I'm completely fucking confused.

"Deacon, I know about the one look thing. The minute I met Michael I felt the same. I was lucky he felt it too."

Fuck, that gets my back up. "Are you saying she doesn't feel it?"

"Oh, she feels it, don't doubt that for one second. Trouble is, when Leia gets all up in her head, she starts to imagine things that aren't happening – like with Charlotte. She'll imagine all sorts of crazy shit. Let me give you some advice, because you're so gone, my friend. If you piss her off, or upset her, only one thing will save your cute ass."

Cute ass? Yeah, I'll let that slide. "What's that?" I have a feeling whatever he tells me may come in handy when I find her.

"*Elvis Presley.*"

"Huh?" Now I'm really fucking confused. What the fuck does a dead singer have to do with anything?

"Leia processes things differently to most people, one of the ways she lets out her feelings is by dancing around in her underwear." He chuckles before going on. "The key to calming her ass down is *The King of Rock 'n Roll*. If she's upset or pissed off, play something by *The King*. There's something in his voice that seems to soothe her soul."

I soak that bit of information in and hope *The King* can help me out this time. I have a feeling, after everything that has happened this past week, Charlotte's shit tonight may have been the last straw.

George pulls up to the front of my place, I look up and notice all the lights are out. I hope to fuck she's sleeping and hasn't left. Climbing from the car, I reach to close the door when Georgie speaks.

"Good luck, Deacon, and remember *The King* will save your cute ass." He laughs, I shut the door on his smug face and watch as he drives away to fetch Michael and Mathew from the hospital. Caroline is staying the night with Jim and asked if Mathew could stay with the boys. He was going to stay with Leia and I, but when Caroline heard what had happened, she told me to concentrate on fixing things between us. I watch as George's car turns the corner and mumble to myself about what a smug bastard he is as I make my way to the door.

~*~

I enter the quiet house and head to the living room, Leia's laptop on the coffee table tells me she's still here. I grab the charging cable for my phone from the low-boy cabinet, Leia's iPod and head upstairs. Before heading to the master bedroom, I step into the bathroom and have a quick shower. Remnants of Jim's blood, which I missed washing away earlier, swirls down the drain. I breathe a sigh of relief knowing he's still alive. I know he's not out of the woods yet, but he's at least alive and that's what matters at this point. Finishing off in the bathroom, I pick up my clothes and throw them into the washing basket by the door before heading towards my room. Coming to a stop at the end of my bed, I watch the rise and fall of Leia's chest as she sleeps and the look of content on her beautiful face. Moonlight streams through the window, illuminating her form, my breath hitches, she's my angel.

Padding silently around the bed, I place Leia's iPod into the dock on the nightstand. I flick through the songs until I find the perfect one and hit play, hoping to god George wasn't lying. *Don't Be Cruel* by *Elvis Presley* plays. Sitting on the side of the bed, I lean over and kiss her lips before trailing a path down her neck. She groans and wriggles as my five o'clock shadow tickles her skin. Sliding a strap of her singlet shirt down, I set one breast free and swirl my tongue around the hard peak of her nipple before sucking it into my mouth and releasing it with a small pop. I move to her other nipple and give it the same treatment. Her hands slide into my hair and her body arches towards me. I sense without looking up, she's awake. After blowing gently over her nipple, I look up and meet hooded, hazel eyes full of heat. I slide back up her body, feathering her with kisses and move so I can brace a hand on either side of her head. She spreads her legs and I fit perfectly between them. Through my towel, I can feel the heat of her pussy pressed against my aching cock, but before I take what I want, I need her to understand it's only her, and it will only ever be her.

I move close to her ear and whisper, "Leia, it's only you babe, it will only ever be you. I don't share myself and I sure as fuck ain't gonna share you so, you better get that through your pretty little head."

"Just you and me," she breathes out and I nod. "I can live with that." She wraps her arms around my neck and steals my breath with a deep kiss causing me to groan in the back of my throat.

"Fuck me," she says breathlessly after ending the kiss.

Her nails travel down my chest causing me to suck in a deep breath. I hiss as she frees my cock from the towel and caresses it. Sitting back on my heels, not wasting any more time, I push her panties to one side and line myself up. Using her wetness, I coat myself, and not being able to resist any longer, I enter with one hard thrust. Her throbbing pussy squeezes around me and we both groan.

"Pure fucking ecstasy, every fucking time, babe," I pant, thrusting in and out, she matches my every move. Reaching forward I place my hand at the base of her throat and feel her pulse increase as her pussy squeezes me, I swear I go crossed eyed. "Fuck, babe, is there anything you don't like?" Fuck, she is a little minx and fuck, that turns me on even more. Leaning down I take her lips in a hard kiss before pulling back and telling her how I really feel, a whisper away from the sweetest lips I have ever tasted. "I love you, Leia."

I watch as her eyes widen and a gorgeous smile spreads across her face, she whispers back, "I love you too."

Damn, hearing that did some funny shit to my heart. "Mine," I growl as I thrust harder, deeper, and trail my hand down to find her clit. Pinching and rubbing, I bring her towards climax. I won't last much longer and I need her to get there before I let go.

"Yours," she pants as sweat coats her skin, her body tenses and she finally gives me what I want. Her pussy clenches and throbs, pushing me over the edge and we both moan as we explode together.

"Fuck, I love you, baby." I devour her lips in a passionate kiss.

"I love you, Deacon."

I roll to the side and take her with me, not willing to break the connection we have. I kiss the top of her head.

"Elvis? Babe, really?" She giggles into my chest as I run my fingers down her back and feel her shiver.

"It suited the moment," is all I say, not wanting to explain the conversation I had with George in the car on the way home.

"Good choice, babe." She kisses my chest before speaking again, she senses I'm exhausted. "Get some sleep, we'll talk in the morning."

I nod, my eyes become heavy, but my last thought almost causes a groan. Fuck, now I owe George big time for saving my ass tonight.

"I love you," she whispers and I feel her breath skim over my heated chest. Her words soothe me, and I know whatever I owe George is well worth it to have this moment with my woman.

Chapter Eighteen

Leia

Using tongs, I flip the bacon as it sizzles and pops in the pan on the stove and crack open an egg into a pan next to it while swaying my hips to *Over And Over* by *Nelly ft. Tim McGraw.* I sing the beautiful lyrics to the song, getting swept away until arms wrap around my waist from behind bringing me back to what I'm supposed to be doing.

"Babe, you know what those hips do to me when you move them like that."

A shiver runs through me as Deacon's voice travels straight to my core, I shake my ass into his front making him growl and nip my ear.

"Tease," he hisses and pulls back, swiping a piece of bacon as he goes.

"Hey, it's not ready yet," I complain. I swing around pouting and he winks at me as he throws it into his mouth. I laugh when he yelps because he's burnt his mouth.

"Haha, Karmas a bitch you know." I smirk at him before turning back to concentrate on the eggs. A sharp slap stings my ass and I moan at the contact.

"Behave, baby," he whispers in my ear.

I shrug from his hold and cross to the fridge to grab the orange juice. Looking over my shoulder, I lick my lips. He's leaning against the bench wearing only a pair of low slung jeans and his arms are crossed over his bare, broad chest. I stare as his muscles flex. *Fuck my man is sexy.*

"We have company behave," I growl before moving to the table so he doesn't see me trying to squeeze my legs together at the sudden ache which has hit me.

I smile to myself at how this man affects me, remembering how he came home from the hospital two nights ago and played me Elvis before confessing he loved me. Just thinking about it now has the ache getting worse. I recall the following morning, we sat down and spoke. He explained about Charlotte and I believed him of course. He reassured me that I was it for him and nothing, or no-one, would ever change that. After we spoke, we dressed and headed into the hospital, it's what we've been doing for the past couple of days - eating, talking and going to the hospital. Then, we come back here, fall into bed and he shows me his love by devouring my body.

~*~

This morning the mood is a little brighter with Georgie, Mickey and Matthew being here for breakfast before we all make the trek up to the hospital. They have been turning the oxygen to Jim's breathing tube down a little at a time and doctors are confident he'll be able to breathe on his own once it's removed. Some of Deacon's worry has washed away as his partner seems to be hanging in there, but he's nervous about this morning. He's going to be brought out of the coma and if all goes well, the breathing tube will be removed. We have been told it may take a while for him to regain consciousness, so there could be a long wait, but we want – no, we need to be there when it happens. I'm not exactly sure about how the case is going, Deacon explained how he was off the case now and it worried me at first, I didn't like to think I was affecting his career and causing him to step outside protocol by being involved with a victim. He said it was okay because now he was on leave he could stay with me and protect me. I liked that idea. Last night, two new detectives showed up to talk to me and Deacon didn't leave my side for a second. So that brings us to now having breakfast before we head back to the hospital.

"Babe, where did you go just now?" Deacon steps up behind me, I jump as he startles me.

"Just thinking about today." I cross to the stove and notice Deacon has removed the eggs.

"It's going to be fine."

I note a hint of uncertainty in his voice and I'm sure he spoke the words for his benefit as well as mine.

"I know."

"Can I ask you something?" Deacon asks as *My Place* by *Nelly ft. Jaheim* begins.

I hum the words and nod towards Deacon.

"Why the fuck are we listening to *Nelly*?" I laugh at the face he pulls.

"What's wrong with *Nelly*?" I ask pretending to be shocked that he doesn't like him.

"Babe, *Elvis* is *The King* and he's my man, the other old school music you play seems to flow like it belongs, like you." He winks at me.

Oh, did I forget to mention, he told me when I asked about going home that this was my home so, why would I want to go anywhere else? Subtle I know, but that's my man for ya.

"*Nelly* is cool, man, don't be dissing my man." I try to act serious and apart from the waving hands, I throw in a head bob which causes him to break into laughter.

I roll my eyes at his ass, plate up the food and carry it to the table.

"I let Mathew pick what he wanted to listen to, hence *Nelly*."

"Okay, I get that, but why is *Nelly* even on your iPod?"

"Because I like *Nelly*. You know that song *Hot in Herre*?"

"Yeah."

His voice is all husky, so I lower my voice and try to make it as seductive as possible when I speak next, "I might show you some sexy moves to that song when we get home tonight, *if* you're lucky and shut your mouth right now about *Nelly*."

"*Nelly* is cool, we should listen to more of him. We can always handle a bit of a change around here." He looks me up and down, licking his lips before swallowing hard and making me laugh. My man has a dirty streak.

~*~

Deacon

Fuck the way she lowered her voice and spoke all husky

made me about come in my jeans. Then, her sexy laugh ricocheted straight through my body, directly to my cock. Imagining her teaching me sexy moves, has my dick leaking in anticipation. Fuck, I need to change the subject, have a cold shower, something, anything, before I say fuck breakfast, throw her ass over my shoulder and take her to our room. I'd spank that ass, oh she wasn't fooling anyone earlier, I heard the quiet moan when I spanked her before and I didn't miss the way she looked at me from the fridge while she squeezed her thighs together. I was fucking glad I wasn't the only one affected at that moment.

Georgie calls out from the back porch and my thoughts return to the present.

"Babe, can you take the plates out back, please," Leia says from the stove.

I shake my head, happy to do something besides stand there gawking. Yeah, I know I was because Leia winks at me knowingly. Fuck.

"Yeah babe, I'm on it." I grab two plates from the table and as I head toward the back door, I hear Leia laughing in the kitchen. Fuck, it's a sexy sound. I want to kick everyone out, take my girl upstairs and show her exactly what she does to me.

After placing the plates down on the outside table, I head back in to grab glasses and the orange juice. Leia walks down the hall carrying the last of breakfast and I can't help but stare as she swings those fucking hips again. *Fuck, she's trying to kill me!*

I move to the table, pull out her chair and grab the remaining plates out of her arms so she can take a seat. I sit after setting the plates on the table. Leia reaches over, grabs the tongs and starts putting food on everyone's plates. It feels so natural for her to be here with me, I hope she understands how serious I was when I told her this was now her home.

Conversation flows and we all dig in while it's hot, but I'm anxious to get to the hospital. I've been nervous all morning even though Leia has done her best to distract me. The doctors said Jim is doing better than expected but have warned, there's still a long road ahead. They said, looking to breathe on his own so soon is nothing short of a miracle, but, I know my partner, he won't give up without a fight. It's knowing that which keeps me sane. Leia notices I've zoned out, gives my hand a squeeze and shoots me a soft smile. I squeeze her hand back, get stuck into my food and listen to George tell Mathew about a trip he and Michael took to Queensland a year ago.

~*~

Two hours later we enter the hospital and head towards the ward where Jim's room is, having him in a private room is good because there are quite a few of us. We kind of overrun the private room as it is let alone putting him a shared space where we'd be forced to share with other visitors.

"Morning, Caroline." Leia walks over and they wrap their arms around each other. Once they step apart, Mathew hugs his mother, pats his dad's hand and says something in his ear.

"Has the Doctor been in yet?" I ask

"Yeah, he just left. He switched off a heap of machines and removed the breathing tube. Apparently, he's breathing well on his own now so there's no need for it. Monitors are still connected so if something goes wrong, alarms will sound." She points to a young doctor who is checking a monitor. "Dr. Roland is his resident and will keep an eye on progress. Now, we wait." Caroline sits in a chair and takes Jim's hand.

I acknowledge the young man when he nods at me, lean against the bed and study the different wires coming out of Jim. There's a drip in his hand and various monitors beep steadily.

I'm not sure how long we sit there, it could have been one

hour or six, but I wasn't leaving the room until he woke up.

George, Michael and Mathew stand and announce they're going to get something to eat and drinks for everyone. As soon as the door closes, Caroline whispers, "Deacon." Her eyes are filled with tears. "You know if he doesn't wake up….." a tear slides down her cheek.

I stand, lift her from the chair and pull her into my arms. "Shhh, you don't have to say anything." She grips my shirt in her hands tighter.

"I do, so listen to me." She's trying to be tough with me but her words don't have the force they usually have.

I nod at her.

"If Jim doesn't wake up, you need to know he loved you like a son."

My heart squeezes in my chest and I open my mouth, not sure what to say, when I hear a whispered scratchy voice from my side.

"Love, don't tell him lies and Deacon, get your fucking hands off my wife."

"Jim!" Caroline yelps, dashes to his side, lifts his hand, careful not to bump the IV taped there and brings it to her cheek.

"Fuck you're a sight for sore eyes, love," he whispers making Caroline giggle.

"Don't you *ever* scare me like that again." She leans forward and kisses his forehead, love shines from her eyes.

"I'll try not to, love," he croaks out.

I move to the other side of the bed, pour him a cup of water and place a straw in it causing him to raise an eyebrow at me.

"Pretend you're on holiday and it's a fucking pina colada, or some shit, and use the friggen straw.”

Caroline raises the bed a little so he can take a few sips.

“I see your attitude still sucks,” he chuckles and fuck if it isn’t good to hear him busting my balls again.

“Well, I haven’t had your ass riding it to keep it in check.”

“Where’s your woman?” he demands to know before smirking at me when Leia comes to my side and smiles down at him

“It's so good to see you awake, you gave us a terrible fright.”

“You too, Leia, but do me a favor and hit him for handling my woman,” he croaks out making us all laugh. Then, I grunt and rub my side after she elbows me causing Jim to chuckle and wince.

“I like her,” he sighs.

“Okay, that’s enough fun, honey, you need your rest.” She bends forward and kisses his forehead again and whispers she loves him.

Jim lays back, closes his eyes, whispers he loves her too and says he wants to see his boy next time he opens his eyes.

Wrapping my arms around my girl, I feel lighter knowing he woke up and still has his smartass attitude, it’s like everything feels better and right. Now we need to find Pete and everything will be right with the world again. Then, me and my woman can get on with our lives, fuck, I'd be lying if I said I didn't look forward to that.

Chapter Nineteen

Leia

Have you ever been afraid of your own shadow? It's not a nice feeling, being terrified that one wrong move could pull you into darkness, to me it would be nothing short of hell. Imagine, nothing but a sliver of light cast upon the floor, the only thing you see, and will ever see are the endless shadows. You can call for help, scream and cry until you have nothing left, until you are a mess on the floor. Begging to capture the dimmest of light, but nothing and nobody, ever comes to save you. It's like the shadows mock you until you slowly go insane.

The endless nightmare plays in my head, over and over, night after night. I wake with a start, tears streaming down my face, cold and shivering. Then, I feel the warmth of Deacon's arms around me, he centers me, calms me. His whispered words in my ear settle my breathing, but as much as I try, I can never fall back to sleep. I lay my head against Deacon's warm chest and let the rise and fall of his muscles soothe me as I battle the inner turmoil which plays inside me every night. I stare out the window and watch as the moon dips low before the sun rises and I smile, hoping the new day will be the one where I stop fearing my own shadow.

~*~

Deacon runs his fingers through my hair and massages my head causing a moan to slip free from my lips. I run the tip of my finger over his muscular six pack and watch as small goosebumps break out. His muscles flex with arousal and they're not all that flexes. I kiss a trail down his abs and move my body until I'm between his legs. When I glance up, I see his soft green eyes staring back at me. I pull the sheet down, exposing his hard cock to me. I lower my head and lick my lips before wrapping my hand around the hard muscle. I flick him with my tongue and when I glance back up, I see his eyes have turned a darker shade of green. Leaning down I swipe the tip with my tongue savoring the salty taste and causing him to groan. I slide my hand up and down, giving a little squeeze every now and then as I suck the tip into my mouth. When I swirl my tongue around him, he groans loudly and pushes himself further into my mouth.

Sliding my hand down, I cup his balls while taking him all the way into the back of my throat and then draw back. I continue this until I feel Deacon wrap my hair in his hand and place it at the top of my head. I look up, lock eyes with him and moan around his cock before sliding it to the back of my throat again. He bucks against me and moans.

"Babe," he pants. "Fuck."

Taking that as a good sign, I speed up my movements and taste more of him as his pre-cum coats my tongue. I moan and feel his balls draw up, his breathing becomes ragged.

"Fuck." He grips my head harder, sending a prickling sensation down my back. "I can't hold back," he grits out between clenched teeth. We lock eyes again and I increase my efforts, bringing my hands up, I grip his hips and apply pressure with my nails as I suck hard. He hisses out curse words as he erupts and pours cum down my throat. I swallow it down not wanting to waste a drop. When he's done, I lick him clean which results in his cock jumping with interest and loud moans to escape.

"Come here, babe." He starts to hook me under the arms to slide me up his body, but I escape his hold and jump off the bed. I grab a change of clothes from where they are packed away in his closet.

"Where are you going?" he growls.

"I have to have a shower, Georgie will be here soon."

"Babe, come back to bed you still have…." he pauses and I assume he's looking for the time. "About an hour."

"Deacon, it takes me more than hour to get ready."

"Put on a paper bag, it won't matter, you would still be as sexy as fuck," he groans before mumbling something under his breath which I don't quite catch. It makes no difference, right now I need a shower.

"Would love to stay and play, but I need a shower." I smile over my shoulder as I head from the room and head to the bathroom. I hear Deacon stomping down the hall and squeal when he races into the bathroom before I have a chance to close the door.

"What are you doing?" I ask in mock displeasure.

He wiggles his eyebrows at me with a mischievous smile on his face. "I want to make you good and dirty before I get you nice and clean." He bends over, throws me over his shoulder and I giggle. I wriggle around until he smacks my ass, making me moan.

"Fuck yeah, babe, that's what I want to hear." Then, he demands, "shower now babe, I have a need to mark you."

The way he says that has my nerve endings firing and my pulse picks up speed. I've totally forgotten why I was in a hurry to shower, my mind is only on this moment as he slides me down his hard body until my toes touch the floor. Before I can suck in a deep breath, he takes my mouth in a kiss which has my toes curling and my legs shaking.

I'm spun around to face the shower wall and place the palms of my hands on the cool tiles. I arch my body, stick out my ass and give it a shake. Deacon growls and I giggle. Then, he slaps my ass not once, but three times, turning my giggles into a moan. He runs fingertips down the middle of my back while his other hand massages away the sting from the slaps, I melt into him. Reaching around he rubs my hard clit until my legs shake uncontrollably, I whimper when he stops the movement and he chuckles. The head of his hard cock rubs against me, I moan when he pushes into me causing us both to groan out in pleasure.

"Every. Fucking. Time. Babe."

All I can do is nod as he increases his thrusts. With one hand on my hip keeping me in place, he grabs a fist full of my hair and pulls my head back, my ass pushes against him. My legs shake, our moans echo around us, I'm nearly there so, I push back to take more of him. A sharp sting to my ass has me tensing up and diving head first over the edge, screaming his name. Two more thrusts and Deacon follows me over. Soft kisses on my neck bring me back to earth, my legs have turned from shaking to jelly.

"I love you, babe," he whispers in my ear.

"I love you too," I breath out as I wait for my racing heart to calm.

~*~

Deacon

Leaving Leia to get dressed in the bathroom, I throw on a pair of jeans and head downstairs for coffee. I smile to myself, I still can't believe I managed to find a unicorn. A woman who can put up with my moody ass, as Caroline puts it. Leia is one of a kind, to look the way she does and still be down to earth, it blows my mind. I love her for the way she allows me to take control in the bedroom and loves everything I do to her, it's sexy as fuck. I get hard just thinking about what else she'll let me do to her. Seeing my handprint on her ass had my possessiveness kicking into full gear. Haha, I want to beat my chest and say 'Me Tarzan, You Jane,' talk about Caveman. I know it's irrational to think that way, but I can't help it. Leia is mine and I'll shout it to the world so everyone understands not to fuck with her.

A knock at the front door has me changing direction, I pull it open to find George and Mathew. I raise my chin in greeting to George and as he enters the house, he returns it. I study Mathew's face as he passes me, I've noticed how quiet he's been lately. He's barely said a word and I'm not sure it's all about his dad. I might get him to stay here while Leia and George head back to her place, no, her *old* place, to grab more of her things.

I close the front door and lead the boys to the kitchen.

"Morning guys, I was about to put the kettle on, want a cup?"

George nods and they follow me into the kitchen. Matthew heads to the fridge, grabs the orange juice and pours himself a glass before he heads to Leia's iPod to search through her music. I notice George watching him too and I raise an eyebrow.

"Has he been like this since his dad went into hospital?"

George speaks quietly, "yeah he hasn't said much, he and Michael have been playing the *Xbox* and talking a little, but he doesn't say much."

"Leave him here while you take Leia to her old place and I'll speak with him."

"So, she agreed to move in?"

"It was going to happen sooner or later, I prefer sooner and Leia didn't argue." I move to the sink, grab a cup, fill it with water and pour it into Elvis's water bow. He waddles over and starts licking it up, I pat his head and laugh.

"Funny?" George cocks an eyebrow.

"I was just thinking, I can't wait for Elvis to grow bigger so I can train him to attack guys who want to hit on my girl."

George laughs. "Yeah, I can see Leia loving that."

I pat Elvis again before I straightening up. "I'll feed you soon, buddy."

Matthew starts *Country Grammar* by *Nelly* playing on the iPod and I shake my head at the boy's music choice. I think I need to have a chat with him about his music choices, but maybe it isn't so bad. Images of Leia doing a strip dance for me the other night comes to mind and I suppress a moan. Fuck, the way she moved her body had me hard as fuck, now, just the image has me *rising* again. Moving back to the kettle, I take coffee cups down from the cupboard and make coffee to take my mind off the seductive images.

I look over my shoulder when Leia starts singing and she shakes that ass of hers. I chuckle, loving the way she's so relaxed and happy here. I know she's having nightmares every night, but she always bounces back and has a smile on her face. I know it's a show for everyone and when I questioned her about it, she told me it's her way of pushing forward. If it's what she needs to do, so be it. I hope the case comes to a close soon so the fucker is gone and hopefully the nightmares will stop.

"Mathew, I love this song, did you know *Nelly* is my main man?"

I growl and look back over my shoulder, she stares at me before winking. Minx.

"Fucking tease," I mumble and turn away when I feel my cock hardening. Taking a few deep breaths, trying to rein my ass in, I feel her arms wrap around me from behind and her hand brushes over my hardening cock. Fuck. Fuck. Fuck.

"Behave!" I warn in a soft voice meant only for her.

I feel the vibration of her soft laugh against my back. Great. Now I'm hard as fuck. She takes pity on me and helps me out a little by pulling my shirt from my jeans so it covers my cock. I'll make her pay for this later. I smile as I picture her handcuffed to my bed on her knees while I redden her ass.

~*~

Half an hour after Leia and Georgie leave to get her stuff, I'm sitting on the back porch with Mathew looking over the yard, wondering if he'll talk to me.

"Is there anything you need to talk about, bud?" I take a sip of my coffee and don't look at him. It takes him a moment, but he finally speaks.

"Are you going to marry, Leia?"

Okay, definitely not what I was expecting, but I'll follow his lead.

"Yeah, bud. When you find a girl, who knocks you to your knees, one who you know you would do anything for, lay the world at her feet, you never let that go."

He nods seeming to think that over before he speaks again.

"Dad says the same about mum."

"I imagine he does, your father is a wise man."

"I don't know what would have happened to mum if dad hadn't woken up." His voice is so quiet I barely hear him.

I place a hand on his shoulder. "Your mum is strong, don't ever doubt that and she has you. I know you would step up and be there for her if need be, but how do you feel?" I push a little and turn to face him, his eyes are glassy with tears. I turn back to look out at the yard so he doesn't get embarrassed.

"I was scared shitless he wasn't going to make it, but I was trying to be strong for mom like dad would have been. I didn't know how to help her, I didn't want to let her down.""

"Mathew, no one expects you to be strong and you certainly didn't let anyone down."

"Why didn't I know what to do, what to say?"

"Your still young, you were hurting too. It's perfectly normal. I know if it was needed, you would have stepped up, but remember, bud, you have me and Leia, Georgie and Mickey to help you and your mum too. When my dad passed away, I felt the same way, but my mum didn't expect me to be strong for her. Instead, we pushed through together, somehow, you work it out." I turn and face him and make him look into my face. "Mathew, talk about your worries and fears, we all need to do that because if you bottle it up, that shit will destroy you."

"Yeah, I know, I couldn't imagine him not being here anymore and it scared the shit out of me. I'm not ready to step up and take his place, I'll never be able to do that."

"No-one expects you to, the key is support of each other. No-one expects you to take your dad's place. You know you can always talk to me right?"

"Yeah, I just didn't know what to say. I had so much going on in my head and I knew how worried everyone was, you didn't need me being a scared crybaby."

"No matter what, I'm here for you. Never be afraid to discuss how you're feeling. It doesn't make you weak, discussing your fears means you're human."

We sit in silence for a moment and I relax back in my chair, gazing up at the blue sky. Clouds are creeping in and it looks like a storm is approaching.

"So, are you going to make me an uncle soon?"

I laugh and he laughs with me. I feel lighter, less worried about him with the shift in conversation. I picture my girl round with my baby and something settles in my chest, I'm really liking that image.

"I'm working on it, she just doesn't know it yet."

He laughs again.

"Can you do me a favor?"

"Depends on what it is."

"Can you pllllleeeease stop playing that *Nelly* shit, it's starting to do my head in."

"But, Leia and I like *Nelly?*" He chuckles and I shake my head at him.

"I'm going to show you what real music is." I get to my feet, head inside and hit the play button on the outdoor speakers. *Whiskey Girl* by *Toby Keith* plays. This song reminds me so much of Leia. As I make my way out to the back porch, I hear Mathew laughing.

"You and fucking Country music, Deacon." He shakes his head.

I know if his mother was here she'd be scolding him for swearing, but I let it slide, it helps him open up.

"Buddy this is music, unlike that shit you listen to, now get your ass up. I have a ticking sound in my car and your gonna help me find what the hell it is"

He gets to his feet and follows me to the garage. Mathew loves working with his hands, especially on cars, maybe it will give him something else to concentrate on.

Chapter Twenty

Leia

"Babe," Deacon calls from upstairs.

"In the living room," I call back. As much as I love my man, he needs to get his ass back to work because he's driving me nuts. I've been here for almost two weeks and known each other for nearly three weeks. I have to admit, although a lot has happened in those weeks, I wouldn't change any of it if it meant I wouldn't be here. No, sorry, scratch that - I would change my involvement with The Shadow Killer. Deacon finally told me everything about the piece of shit. I was pissed he didn't tell me the full story to begin with, but I understand he was trying to keep me safe. Also, his Lieutenant would have fired him if he'd told me too much about a case he was working on. I pretended I was pissed even so, until he played *Elvis*. I'm pretty sure Georgie told him about my weakness where *The King* is involved, and trust me I will have words with that boy. I glance up from my computer when Deacon appears in the doorway of the living room holding something in his hand.

"What's up Buttercup?" I laugh when he scowls at the pet name.

Since he's been off work and driving me crazy, I decided I would drive him crazy by coming up with a different pet name each day. I'll see which one sticks or, which annoys him the most and file the information away for future reference. Why you ask? Because it amuses me. Yesterday he was Puddin', the day before was Cherry Pie, can you see where I'm going with this? It somehow seems to involve food. At first, Deacon thought I was telling him I was hungry, but he finally clued in and growls every time. The irritation doesn't last long and usually ends well for both of us. I end up flat on my back with him sliding home into what he says is "pure fucking ecstasy." I stare at him, waiting for the growl. Right on cue, it rumbles from his chest and I laugh.

"We're going to discuss you calling me food names, but first we're going to talk about what I just found." He holds up my pillbox and I scrunch up my face, wondering where he found it.

"Where did you find them?" I'm puzzled, I've been looking for it everywhere.

"In the medicine cabinet."

"Well damn, Georgie must have put them there. I usually keep it in my underwear drawer. Does it make you uncomfortable having them in there? I don't understand what you're getting at."

"Babe, you don't need these."

"What do you mean, I don't need them. Not that it matters, I couldn't find them and haven't...." I feel the blood drain from my face when realization hits me. Fuck, I haven't had my pill since before I came here. Shit, how the hell did I forget about them?

"What?" Deacon throws the packet on the table as if in disgust, then he moves closer and squats in front of me. He rubs his hands up and down my thighs.

"Nothing, I'm just gonna call Georgie." I start to stand, but his hands grip my legs so I can't move.

He leans forward and kisses down my neck, sending shivers through my body, making me melt as he hits the sweet spot behind my ear. "Talk to me, babe," he whispers and sucks the lobe into his mouth.

It's like I'm in trance and words start flying out of my mouth, I can't seem to stop them.

"I haven't had my pill since I came here! At first I couldn't find them and then I forgot about them."

"Fuck, yeah!" His lips capture mine and I'm on my back before I have a chance to realize he's moved my laptop. He's between my legs, his hard cock pushed against me. I whimper as he slides his hand down my body and rests it against my belly, he breaks the kiss and gazes into my eyes. "You could be pregnant with my baby!"

All I can do is nod, seeming to have lost all brain function and my mouth doesn't want to work.

"Let's increase the chances." Before I know what's happening, he releases his cock from his jeans, pushes my shorts and undies down my legs and thrusts deep inside me with one hard push. I throw my head back and moan, he bites my neck and licks the sting away as he thrusts in and out. I rake my nails down his naked back causing him to hiss and arch into my touch. He increases his thrusts and our moans echo around us. Then, my body locks up, tenses and I explode as he lets go himself and erupts inside me.

"Babe. Nothing. Fucking. Sexier!" He kisses me again. "Mine!" he growls into my mouth.

I nod and say the one word he likes to hear, "Yours."

~*~

After we catch our breath, he straightens his clothes and helps me to put my shorts back on. He gives me a beautiful smile which has my heart racing all over again. I finally find my voice again.

"You want a baby with me?"

"Babe, I want *everything* with you. Picturing you round with our baby has me wanting to take you up to our room and not let you leave until it's a done deal."

Well fuck me standing, it looks like we're making a baby. "Okay."

"Okay to which part because I'll throw you over my shoulder now and have you on your back in about 2.5 seconds if that's what you mean."

"As much as that is a tempting offer, I think we have to go to the hospital soon. I could already be pregnant so, I'll call Georgie and see if he can stop at the chemist on the way over."

"I'll go to the chemist, but call George and he can stay with you until I get back."

"Are you sure?"

"Babe, you can ask me to buy tampons and I'll do it, so I can grab a damn pregnancy test." He thinks about what he just said for a moment and laughs. "Maybe not the tampons."

I laugh and nod. "Okay caveman, go and get the test and I'll call Georgie." Appearing happy with that, he bends and kisses me again. When he heads upstairs to grab a shirt, I call Georgie. And,

I'd be lying if I said my mind wasn't completely blown right now. A baby? Shit, I know we haven't been together long, and the thought of a baby scares the shit out of me, but I can't help picturing Deacon with a baby in his arms and I want that, I really do.

~*~

Deacon

An hour after leaving Leia with George, I stride into the grocery store and straight toward the aisle where the condoms are stacked. Wait a minute, no, I haven't reconsidered. It's the same aisle where the pregnancy kits are kept. I know this because I use to laugh about the fact they are beside each other on the shelf with headache tablets alongside. It's a case of – 'wrap it or buy the test.' It used to scare the shit out of me, that one day I might have to buy a pregnancy test so I've always wrapped it. But, today I feel kind of proud about buying the test. Hmmm, what do they say – 'pride goes before a fall?' Yep, I fell, every fucking type of fucking pregnancy test known to man is on the shelf in front of me. I study the boxes and drag my fingers through my hair. Why the hell are there so many choices? Some say they're 95% accurate, others 99%. Well shit, I want one that will give us the most accurate result so, I grab the last three 99% accurate boxes from the shelf. If we're not pregnant this time, having some on hand will save me the time of coming here every goddam day. I resolve to keep her ass in bed until she's pregnant, not that she's out of bed very often these days.

My phone vibrates in my back pocket, I take it out and find Jacobs' name flashed on the screen. I hope he has something good to tell me about the case. Even though I'm off the case, he's a good man and rings to both keep me informed and pick my brains. We still can't work out what the hell the thirteenth key opens.

"Jacobs?" I answer.

"Black, we have a lead on where to find Pete."

"About fucking time."

"Only because his sister, Charlotte, heard from him and contacted us immediately. We're about to move on him, I thought you would appreciate a call. If it wasn't for you and Barnes we wouldn't have his sister."

"Let me know when you have him custody." I'll breathe easier knowing he's behind bars. I would have preferred the son of a bitch in a body bag, but a jail cell is better than nothing.

"Will do." He ends the call and I slide the phone back into my pocket.

I make my way to the chocolate aisle and grab something for Leia. I learnt my lesson the last time I brought her flowers. She loved them, but when they died, I swear there were tears. After that, she asked if I was to buy her something to make it chocolate because she couldn't handle when the flowers died on her. I didn't hesitate to agree.

Grabbing something for dinner, I head to the register and pay for my purchases. The lady serving looked me up and down as if I was strange when she saw the number of pregnancy tests I was buying. It didn't bother me one bit, seeing my woman round with my baby will be sexy as fuck. I'll start bulk buying the little bastards if at the end of the day, one shows what I want to see. I pay the lady, cross to the car, throw the bags in the trunk and start the engine. As I drive, I flip through the radio stations, settling on one playing country music. I relax in the seat and tap my fingers on the steering wheel to the beat as I make my way home.

~*~

Pulling into the driveway, I shift the car into park and switch off the motor. I jump out and head to the trunk. I'm about to open it and grab the bags when I feel the barrel of a gun pushed into my back. I hear the recognizable click of a gun being cocked. I shake my head in disgust, I should have seen this shit coming. I knew tracking this fucker down and having him in a jail cell by the end of the day was too simple. Yeah, I know who this fucker is. I swing around, come face to face with Pete and notice how strung out he is. His eyes are wild and sweat coats his forehead. I theorize about how to get the gun away from him before he pulls the trigger.

"You tried to hide her from me," he spits.

"Pete, you need to calm the fuck down before you do something stupid."

"Too late for that." His voice is calm, calculated.

The blood freezes in my veins and I start to swing my head towards the house. Leia, fuck!

He pushes the gun into my chest harder and I stay still.

"What the fuck did you do to my girl?" Blood pumps through my veins with the force of a raging river, my heart picks up speed. I'm ready to end this and kill the fucker once and for all when something hits me in the back of the head, pain explodes behind my eyes and darkness descends, but not before I hear a voice I recognize.

"Stop fucking around and take him to the back, we don't have time for this."

Chapter Twenty-one

Leia

What the fuck happened? I remember going to the bathroom and when I walked out, someone grabbed me and covered my mouth with a funny smelling cloth. Now my mouth feels like I swallowed cotton balls. I try to open my eyes, but my head starts to spin so, I concentrate on breathing. When I attempt to move my hands, they're trapped. *What the fuck*? I try again, pulling harder this time, but they're secured tight. I move my feet, they're not tied, a plus in this fucked up situation I guess. "Fuck," I groan. I hear a noise like someone shuffling their feet and freeze in fear, wondering what the hell is going on. Then, I hear a muffled voice from beside me. Cracking my eyes open, I try to see what the noise was. Through blurred vision, I look around and take in my surroundings. I'm in one of our spare bedrooms. Sweeping my eyes to the side, I cry out when I see Georgie tied to a chair with a gag in his mouth.

"Noooo!" Tears flood my eyes.

Georgie shakes his head while he works on getting rid of the gag. He's trying to calm me, I see it in his eyes, but my tears flow. He spits out the gag and speaks softly, "Lee Lee, calm down. Deacon will be back soon, he'll get us out of this."

A noise from the door draws our attention and we both turn our heads. My eyes widen when I see who walks through the door.

"I'm sorry sweetie, Deacon is kind of tied up right now." She laughs like a lunatic.

"What did you do?" I speak through the tears and try to catch my sobbing breath. My stomach clenches at the thought of her hurting my man.

"Oh, sweetie, I haven't done anything. Yet." She winks and the air leaves my lungs.

"Who the fuck are you?" Georgie snarls.

"Who am I?" Charlotte laughs "The newspapers named me The Shadow Killer, it has a nice ring to it don't you think? But, I'm just a poor defenseless woman with a serial killer brother or so everyone thinks."

"You're a sick, twisted bitch," I growl. It doesn't seem to faze her and when she looks over at me, I notice how vacant her blue eyes really are. They're like cold chips of ice, a shiver runs through my body.

"Why are you doing this?" Georgie asks, taking the focus away from me.

I try to wiggle my hands free.

"Why not?" she shrugs. "Sorry, can't talk right now, I have

a detective to have some fun with. I'll leave you both in the hands of my brother, he has something special in store for you, sweet Leia." She moves closer and runs her nails down the side of my face.

I snap my teeth at her, she laughs. I kick out but she moves and I don't connect. *Fuck!*

"You are a feisty one, my brother always likes the feisty ones," she says cheerfully before turning and heading from the room.

"Georgie, I need to get my hands free."

"Keep trying and I'll keep her brother occupied"

"Georgie, we have to get to Deacon." I'm stressed and wriggle my hands violently. The rope loosens and burns my skin, but I grit my teeth and try again. I'll deal with the pain later.

"My beautiful treasure." The voice comes from the doorway, my body locks up as fear shoots through me. The voice from my nightmares has come to life. I look over to the door, a guy leans against the wall with what looks like a voice recorder to his mouth. I take him in from head to toe, he's wearing black cargo pants and a black shirt. He's tall, but not as tall and well-built as Deacon. He holds the recorder away from his mouth and licks his lips before he speaks,

"voice changer."

"It isn't any wonder you need it, you sound like a bitch," Georgie spits out.

I whimper when the guy approaches and slaps him in the face. It doesn't stop Georgie, he continues to bait him and take the attention from me.

"Now I know why you have me strapped to this chair, you slap like a bitch, too." Georgie spits blood at his shoes and I squeeze my eyes shut when the guy pulls back and hits him again.

"Stop! Please stop!" I scream out.

He stops and swings around to glare at me before taking the few steps separating us. He stands off to one side so I can't reach him with my legs and trails a hand down my body. My stomach churns at his touch.

"Don't fucking touch her, you piece of shit. You want to be a man, come here."

I'm trying to figure out what Georgie is trying to do and then I remember what he said before this guy walked in. I begin to pull on the rope again when he turns away from me. I squirm and twist my hands until I feel the rope give a little more, blood slides from my fingers as the rope cuts into me.

"Let me guess, your pussy ass deals with the girl, while your sister takes on the man. How fucking noble," Georgie taunts.

I see the guy pull a knife from the waistband of his pants, it's now or never, I can't allow him to hurt Georgie. I pull hard one last time and one of my hands slips free. It's enough for me to swing my body around and without thinking, I kick him in the back. He stumbles, loses his footing and crashes to the floor hitting his head. I quickly free my other hand and jump to my feet. I sway a little from the effects of whatever they knocked me out with. I stumble to Georgie, untie the ropes and free his hands. I bend to get the ropes at his feet, but I'm wrenched back by my hair and scream when a knife is pushed to my throat. He drags me to my feet and wraps his arm tightly around me.

"Bitch, you'll die for that."

I swallow hard and brace myself. Then, with all my strength, I kick back, hitting him straight in the balls. It gives me enough time to push out of his hold, but I feel the knife slice my throat and scream out. When I place my fingers to the cut, I find it's not deep.

I watch as Georgie dives for him and takes him to the

ground. They roll around on the floor exchanging blows, I see the glint of the knife on the floor, reach for it and pick it up. When the guy is on top, I plunge the knife deep into his back. He screams and arches against the pain. I pull the knife out and thrust it in, over and over. Blood pools around him and seeps into the carpet. I think about the mess I'll have to clean up. *Fuck! I think the craziest shit at the craziest times.*

Georgie gently takes the knife from my shaking hands. "It's okay, Babygirl. He's done."

I nod as he gathers me into his chest and I breath him in. Easing back, he lifts my head and examines my neck.

"I think he just nicked me," I reassure him.

He opens his mouth to say something, but we hear Deacon yelling. Without a second thought, I take off running with Georgie hot on my heels. I search everywhere in the house, but I can't find him. Fear grips me and tears start run down my face. I'm desperate to get to him, worried I won't find him in time.

~*~

Deacon

Leia's screaming penetrates my foggy brain. It takes me a minute to realize I can't move my hands or feet because I'm tied to a fucking chair. I can't believe I let that bitch get the better of me and why the fuck didn't I clue in that she was involved all along. Stevenson said Pete had a partner, but we automatically thought it was that asshole, Donald. We made the mistake of not making sure it was him. Working with the Detective unit, I should have known it wasn't a forgone conclusion that it was Donald. I look around and survey my surroundings, I'm in my garage. I glance down and notice my shirts gone and I'm wearing only my jeans. I swing around when I hear Charlotte's voice from the doorway.

"Good, you're finally awake, I was starting to think you were going to miss all the fun."

"You stupid bitch, what the fuck do you think you're doing? If you think you can get away with this..."

She throws back her head and laughs like a maniac and it grates down my back like razors. I'm wondering again, why didn't we see how psycho this bitch was when we first met her?

"I've been getting away with this for over six years, you lot are fucking clueless." She smiles and shakes her head at me like I'm a complete idiot as she slowly approaches.

It hits me like a ton of bricks. Fuck! "You're The Shadow Killer."

"Well, well, well. Finally. You're not a very smart detective, it took you long enough to figure this shit out. Pity, you won't be able to stop me. You see, when I've had some fun, I'm going to kill you and the rest of your men still won't have a clue it's me."

I think about that for a minute and decide to play her game. I'm going to play dumb to get the information I need from this bitch.

"So where does your brother fit in to all of this?"

"Oh, trust me he had a say. He got to pick the girl he wanted to have. My brother isn't very smart and is shy around women, so I had to help him out."

Is she saying she did all this to get her brother laid, yeah, I'm not buying that bullshit for a second.

"By killing people?"

"See I knew you would zero in on that little detail, detective. I guess you're not as stupid as I thought, I guess that's how you made detective, by not missing details. Well, except for me of course." She winks and steps over to my workbench where she runs her fingers over my tools. Some have been lined up, she obviously did it while I was knocked out.

"So, tell me why did you kill them?"

"I've always wanted to know what it felt like to take somebody's life, but I didn't realize how euphoric it would feel, watching the life drain from someone. It's quite a powerful feeling, holding somebody's life in your hands, watching as a thousand emotions play over their face. It's quite beautiful and ever since the first kill, I guess it became addictive. I kept wanting to do it over and over." She speaks as if taking a life isn't a big deal, I guess to her, it isn't. She slowly moves towards me with a blowtorch in her hand. She flicks it on.

"I think that's enough talking for now."

"Why, we were becoming such good friends," I manage to grit out through clenched teeth as she waves the torch over my arm and I'm gripped by pain. I shout curse words at the top of my lungs, my head spins and swirls as pain sears my arm. I feel faint and the smell of burnt flesh creeps up my nose, causing my stomach to turn.

"I told you we'd have fun, my, my, I didn't know so many curse words existed." She laughs as she switches it off.

I grunt and try to push past the burning pain in my arm. I drop my head in an attempt to stop it spinning.

"You're right, we were becoming good friends. How rude of me, what else would you like to talk about?" Her voice is cheery, ignoring the fact she was burning my skin off a second ago.

I lift my head and watch as she crosses to the bench again. She places the torch down, picks up a screwdriver and weighs it in her hand before coming back to me.

I flex my hands and pain shoots up my arm. I grit my teeth through the pain and flex my hands. When I hear the wooden chair creak under the strain of me pulling against it, I wonder if I'd be able to break it.

"Tell me about the keys," I grunt out in an attempt to divert her attention.

"You already know about twelve of them. I'm sure you were smart enough to work out, the names matched each woman my brother chose. It's the thirteenth key you're wondering about, isn't it?"

I nod, no point beating around the bush. She knows what I want to know and I hope to fuck she tells me, even if it's the last thing I ever hear. I need to know the missing piece of this puzzle.

"As I said, my brother isn't a smart man. He decided to get Donald involved to help drug the girls, but he also decided to keep each key as a trophy and gave them to his scumbag mate. I told him he was to get rid of them, but he ignored me. You're puzzled because the thirteenth key was blank." She stops and I don't think she is going to say anything else, but she continues after a moment. "Hmmm, since you're going to die today, I may as well tell you the story. So, tell me detective, when you searched Donald's girlfriend's place, did you happen to check the backyard?"

What the fuck has his backyard got to do with anything? There was nothing besides an old shed. Forensics went through it and there was nothing there. She must have noticed my confusion and she leans over and runs her nails down the side of my face. Then, she leans real close until she is a breath away from my lips and locks eyes with me, they're the coldest eyes I have ever had the misfortune to look into. The next thing I scream out FUCK! as she stabs me in the thigh with the screwdriver.

"Poor baby, did that hurt?" She smirks, grabs the handle of the screwdriver and yanks it out, causing me to yell out again. "What else do you want to know?" She returns to the workbench and picks up a hammer.

I wheeze out in pain and feel the wetness of blood as it runs down my leg. Fuck, this bitch is nuts. I hear Leia's screams coming from inside the house and forget about the pain. I try hard to free myself, but it's no fucking use, I'm well and truly secured. I groan in pain as images of what's happening to my girl bombard my mind and I can't do jackshit about it. I close my eyes, and picture her beautiful face. I hope to God I can get to her soon.

"Sounds like my brother is having fun." Charlotte breaks into my thoughts and I look over to see her place the hammer back on the bench and pick up a pair of pliers. She paces in front of me. "When I get free, I'm going to make you wish you'd never been born."

"Detective, I already wish that" Stopping she leans over and pushes her finger into the wound left by the screwdriver causing me to scream out again, seeming satisfied she goes back to pacing again "So moving along, is there anything else that you want to know?"

"Why a circle?" I feel my hand slip free from the rope and flex it to get the circulation going again. Then, I concentrate on trying to get the other one free. She stops again, looks at me thoughtfully, squats in front of me. All the time she plays with the pliers in her hand.

"That was just for fun. I thought, why not make a pattern? I knew Donald would eventually become a problem so, I used the place he shared with his girlfriend as my guideline and went from there. But, the ingenious part was, my dad's shop is smack bang in the middle of the circle."

Holy fucken shit!

Something must be showing on my face because hers lights up like a fucking christmas tree.

"I know, right? And, it wasn't even planned." She gets to her feet. "Okay, I think I've answered all your questions now." She pulls her hand back and attempts to hit me in the side of the head with the pliers, but I'm quicker. I shoot my hand out and grip her wrist, stopping her movement. Her eyes widen and a flicker of fear flashes across her face, it's the first emotion I've seen from her today, but it doesn't last long. She lifts her leg and presses her knee into my leg wound, smirking when I yell out, but I don't let go of her wrist.

I hear a loud bang and look to the garage door as it flies open, my girl is standing there with my fucking gun raised and aimed at Charlotte. I look her over and see she's covered in blood. Fuck!

"Get the fuck away from my man and don't move," Leia screams. Yeah, she said that and even fucked up right now, her words shot straight to my dick.

I push Charlotte away, George comes in behind Leia, heads straight to me and starts undoing the ropes.

"Can you walk?" George asks.

I nod, grit my teeth and attempt to stand. My ass hits the chair again and I have to take few deep breaths as my head spins.

"I've got you, mate." George wraps an arm around me just as the gun goes off. *What the Fuck?* Getting to my feet with George's help, I look towards Charlotte on the ground and watch as blood pools around her. I turn to my woman and she shrugs.

"She moved."

George chuckles and I join him. The jury is out on whether or not she actually did move.

"Are you hurt, babe?" I look closely at the blood covering her before she races over to me and wraps her arm around my waist, taking some of my weight.

"It's not my blood." She raises her free hand to her neck. "This is just a nick."

"Babe, we need to call this in."

"Already done and an ambulance is on its way," George says.

We make our way out to the driveway and I hear the sirens in the distance.

Chapter Twenty-Two

Leia

I stand close and watch as Deacon is lifted into the back of the ambulance. I feel like I'm floating, looking down on everything that's happening. It's all so surreal. Adrenaline drains from my body and I'm trembling when George wraps his arms around me. I look up and see darkening bruises marring his beautiful face, and dried blood seals the cut on his lip.

"I need to go with him," I tell Georgie.

He nods and guides me to the ambulance. Georgie helps me into the back and I sit where I'm told to while a paramedic works on stopping the blood flow from the wound on Deacon's leg. I see the terrible burns on his arm and wonder if he'll need a skin graft.

Tears roll over my cheeks, it's all my fault. Deacon and Georgie wouldn't have been hurt if it wasn't for me.

"Leia!"

Deacon's sharp tone draws my attention.

"It's not your fault, babe. I'm here and alive because of you, babe."

How the fuck does he know what I'm thinking? I reach over to his outstretched hand and grasp his warm fingers. He's alive and he's okay, I tell myself. I don't know what I would have done if that bitch had killed him, how I would have gone on. I'm not sorry I shot and killed her, she deserved it – retribution on behalf of all the people she killed. My eyes widen when I hear Deacon giving orders to one of the medics.

"You need to check my girl over, I can wait. Take care of her, she's bleeding and in shock."

The Paramedic shakes his head. "Detective, we'll take care of her as soon as we have your bleeding under control." He glances at me and I nod. I only have a small nick, they need to take care of Deacon first.

"Let them do what they need to do, babe, I can wait." He scowls at me, he doesn't like to be contradicted. "I promise I'll get checked over at the hospital." Deacon stares at me hard and when he sees I'm not wavering from my decision, he nods.

Then, I watch as the blood appears to drain from his face, he's pale as a ghost. His hand becomes slack in mine and his eyes close.

The Paramedic shouts his name over and over, but there's no response. Alarms are sounding on a machine they have him hooked up to. What the fuck is happening?

"Detective, squeeze my hand," the medic shouts.

I watch for any response, nothing. Why won't the fucking machine shut up? The tone changes and the wriggly lines have become one long, flat line. I've watched enough movies to know that's not good. *NO, this can't be happening no… no… no….*"Deacon, open your eyes, babe!"

The medic yells at the driver to get moving then snaps at me, "miss, you need to calm down."

I realize I was shouting and losing my shit so, I apologize and quiet down.

The ambulance screeches to a stop, the doors are ripped open and the gurney is dropped to the ground. The men take off running through the doors to Emergency. I'm frozen in place, I want to run after them but my legs won't work.

Arms wrap around me and I'm pulled back against a hard chest. I start to fight, but Georgie whispers in my ear, telling me to calm down. As much as I want to fight him and run after Deacon, I know he's right. The fight leaves me and I sag into his hold. This can't be happening he was just talking to me, he was fine. What the fuck just happened?

~*~

An hour later we find ourselves in the room where we waited to hear news about Jim. Georgie has been checked over, the doctor said he was okay and wouldn't suffer any permanent damage. I've also been examined and after they cleaned up the wound on my neck, a small plaster was applied.

The two detectives, which had taken over the case from Deacon and Jim, arrived and I gave them my statement. The nurses gave me a pair of scrubs to put on as my clothes were needed as evidence, or some shit like that.

So, here I am, pacing up and down this small ass waiting room wondering what the hell is happening with Deacon. Georgie,

Mickey, Mathew and Caroline sit waiting nervously. Apparently, Jim got word about what had happened, no idea how, and sent Caroline up to see how things were going.

The door bursts open. I hold my breath and wait for the Doctor to speak. "Miss James?"

I approach the man. "Yes."

"Detective Black lost a large amount of blood, we've given him three bags and he's stable. He's still in ICU and stable. We expect he'll make a full recovery. A nurse will come by in about an hour and take you in to see him."

I release the breath I'd been holding and tears fall from my eyes. I wipe them away and nod. "That's good, right?" I glance around the room and see the smiling faces of my family. That's what we are - family.

"It's better than good, Babygirl." Georgie holds me to his chest and tears flow, releasing the fear, worry and tension from the day.

"Thank you, Doctor." Georgie says over my head and I hear the door close with a soft click as the Doctor leaves.

"I'll be back in a minute," Caroline says before leaving.

I nod my head into Georgie's chest, trying to get my shit together, but the weight of the day is crashing into me and I can't stop the tears from falling.

By the time Caroline gets back, I have myself together and we decide to grab a coffee while we wait to visit my man. It feels like the walls of this room are closing in on me, I need to escape for a short time.

As we head towards the café, Caroline asks, "how are you feeling sweetie?"

"I don't know," I answer honestly.

"I understand, but our men are strong and they have too much fight in them to let things like this get them down. I organized to have Deacon moved into the same room as Jim so they have each other to talk to."

I think about Jim's room, would there be enough room for another bed? Then I remember another set of oxygen outlets and switches for machines on the far wall where another bed would probably fit. It would be a tight squeeze but the boys will be good for each other.

"Good idea. Tell me, how did you guys know what had happened this morning?"

"Detective Jacobs stopped by this morning and gave Jim his police scanner so he could listen in to their operation. He's not supposed to have it so, if the Lieutenant turns up we need to hide it." She laughs as we step up to the counter. "They must drive their boss crazy with what they get up to."

I laugh with her before placing our order.

~*~

Deacon

Wine colored eyes are all I can see clearly through the fog in my head. A dull, painful throbbing in my leg pulls me from my dream. I blink my eyes open and groan, a beeping sound causes my head to thump. I attempt to focus, everything is fuzzy. As my vision clears, I find myself in a hospital room, the walls are white and everything looks sterile. I hear a chuckle from beside me and look over to find my partner sitting up in bed eating *Jello*.

"What the fuck happened?" I try to sit up, but when I put pressure on my arm, it fucking kills. I look down to see, it's covered in bandages and I remember that bitch burning me. I reach for the remote beside my hand and press the button to raise the back of the bed. I groan with the pain assaulting my body and the stiffness in my back.

"You tryin' to outdo me?" Jim asks.

I give him my best 'what the fuck' glare and he chuckles before wincing in pain.

"Hope that hurt, fucking Karma that was." I smirk at him when he shoots me a 'fuck off' glare.

"Let's face it, you just couldn't handle being away from me, could you? It's very touching to know the lengths you'll go to so you can be with me."

"Yeah, because you're the first fucking person I think about when I open my eyes every morning."

"I know."

"Fucking, dick," I mumble while trying to stretch out the kinks in my body, it fucking hurts like a bitch.

"How the fuck did I end up in a room with your ass?"

"Caroline." One word as if it needs no further explanation and it doesn't. Of course, his wife would put us together. She either thought it would be easier to visit us both, or she is trying to punish me. I'll put money on it being the latter.

"Where's my fucking *Jello*, you greedy bastard?"

"I told the nurse you didn't like it and offered to eat it so it wouldn't be thrown away." He swallows the last mouthful.

"Motherfucker," I growl

"You took my mashed potatoes back at the office, payback's a bitch," he shoots back.

"I would beat your ass right now if I could stand and my fucking arm wasn't killing me, greedy prick."

"Deacon Black!" Caroline chastises me as she enters the room.

My eyes lock on Leia who follows her in. She has the brightest smile on her face as she rushes towards me and I notice how glassy her eyes are, she's been crying.

"He stole my *Jello*," I grumble in my defense, but I don't give two fucks about it now. My girl leans down and presses her lips to mine. I forget all about the *Jello,* my greedy partner and zone out as Caroline rips into Jim about taking my stuff.

"I missed you baby," I whisper into her lips

"I missed you too." Tears fall from her eyes.

Jim snarls, "Caroline, why did you have him moved in here, now I have to listen to his sappy ass?"

"Shut it, Jim, I think it's sweet," Caroline says.

I pull my eyes away from my girl and look over at the pair of them. Caroline has a bright smile on her face and Jim mumbles some shit I don't hear when George, Michael and Mathew walk in. I smile when Mathew walks over with more *Jello* for me.

"I knew dad would eat yours so, I brought you some more," he laughs and places it on my tray.

"Thanks, buddy, you're a better man than your prick of a father." We both laugh and he nods, he knows I'm trying to rile up his father.

"Son, get your ass over here and give me a hug."

I lean back against the pillows and look around the room at our family. I'm exhausted, but fuck I'm a lucky son of a bitch to be surrounded by such good people. I watch them talking to each other before glancing at Jim. He's looking so much better, I watch as he looks at everyone before turning to me and winking.

"Stop checking my ass out, I know I'm handsome, but I'm taken." He takes hold of Caroline's hand.

"Don't worry, mate. I'm good with my girl here." Leia squeezes my hand before my eyes become heavy and I let sleep overtake me. As I drift off, I think about wine colored eyes and a sassy attitude as she whispers in my ear how much she loves me.

Like I said, I'm one lucky son of a bitch.

Epilogue

12 Months later...

Leia

It's been just over twelve months since Deacon came into my life and turned my life upside down, in such a good way. After everything settled down, we still had a long road ahead of us with Deacon and Jim's recovery. It was only a month ago, they were both ready and returned to their jobs as partners.

In reality, Deacon was ready three months ago, but felt he couldn't operate without Jim, a part-time partner didn't sit well. The Doctor's recommended he take the extra time to heal properly so, he was able to go back to work when Jim was ready.

Detectives Jacobs and Ryan returned to Donald's home to try to find something that would explain the thirteenth key. After an intensive search, they found an underground shelter tucked away behind dense brush. It was padlocked and of course, the thirteenth key unlocked it. What they found was the stuff horror movies are made of. Deacon explained it was a shrine to all the past victims and there were images and tapes for another twenty which were planned. I'm guessing there was a lot more, but Deacon didn't want to fill my head with the rest of the shit, his words not mine.

Either Donald or Pete had booby trapped the place so, if someone stumbled across it a timer would count down. Unfortunately, by the time Ryan and Jacobs worked it out, it was too late. They turned to run as the place exploded. Detective Ryan was hit by numerous pieces of shrapnel and died at the scene. Detective Jacobs threw himself to the ground as soon as he cleared the underground space, but the explosion sent him flying into an old car in the backyard and he was left with a badly broken arm.

It was a sad time for everyone, even in death, the scumbags had taken another innocent life. Upon hearing the news, Georgie and Mickey, with the help of Mathew, made a memorial plaque with Ryan's photo displayed in the center. They delivered it to the Detectives unit and a ceremony was held before it was hung on the wall. I attended with Deacon, it was the sweetest gesture and more than a few tears were shed.

~*~

A month after everything began to settle down and we were finally moving forward without fear, Deacon requested, hmmm requested is putting it mildly. Let's say, he demanded I take a pregnancy test, unfortunately it was negative. Deacon then vowed that once he was home, he was going to change that. He made good on his word so, that leads us to where we are now.

I'm a week away from my due date to bring our daughter into the world. I'm relaxing on the porch in the backyard, absently running my hand over my never-ending belly, drinking orange juice and picturing our beautiful little girl growing and playing in the backyard. I smile at the image of her helping her daddy tinker with his car.

"Ahhh shit," I gasp, jerking forward and dropping the glass of juice to the ground. "Fuck. Fuck. Fuck." I grip my stomach and feel my waters break. *Shit, not now.* The sharp pain seems to subside and I push to my feet. When the next pain hits, I breathe through it. Once it passes, I hurry to the kitchen and grab my keys and phone from the kitchen bench thinking I'll phone Deacon on the way. I make it as far as the front door before doubling over in pain. I scream with the agony, take a few deep breaths and try to make it to my car. *I can do this, no need to call anybody. You're just having a baby for fuck sake.* Pain shoots through me, my stomach expands forward and tightens. *I got this shit.* I reach the car and reach to open the door when I hear Georgie calling out to me. I had completely forgotten he was coming over this morning. I turn, push my back against the door of my car, bend forward and grip my knees when another powerful contraction hits.

Georgie sprints over to me. "Fuck, Lee Lee, please tell me you weren't thinking of driving yourself to the hospital." He holds me while I cry out through the next pain so I don't hit the deck.

I nod my head and grit my teeth through the pain.

"Your fucking crazier than I thought, Deacon would kill you."

I growl at his stupid ass as he guides me to the passenger side of the car, stopping a few times on the way as the contractions hit harder and faster. Finally getting my ass in the car, Georgie shuts the door and runs around the front of the car with his phone to his ear. I try to concentrate on him and not the pain. His mouth is going at a hundred miles an hour and he's waving his arms excitedly in the air. After a moment, he shoves the phone in his back pocket and climbs into the car.

"Deacon will meet us at the hospital," he says as he starts the motor.

I nod, not giving a shit right now.

"Breath, Babygirl."

"I'm trying, what the fuck do you think I'm doing!" I scream at him. His eyes widen and his mouths hangs open at my outburst. The expression on his face is quite comical and I would laugh if I wasn't in so much fucking pain right now. I feel the car accelerate and try to breathe through the pain, everything is a blur, we must be travelling fast. I alert him to the fact we're about to pass a speed camera.

"Fuck the camera," he says, but I feel the car slow a little.

Another pain grips me and I breathe deeply. I slam my hands on the dashboard, hang my head and hum as I feel the pain slice up my back. Car tires screech as we stop in front of the doors to the hospital. Georgie flies around the car and rips my door open. He's trying to pull my ass out, but the pain is crippling. I can't move so, he runs inside and grabs one of the wheelchairs they have at the front doors before rushing back to me with a nurse in tow.

"I'm going to try and lift your ass out okay?"

I nod and Georgie places his hands under my arms, lifts me out and turns me to sit in the chair. I hear another car screech to a stop and Deacon calls my name. I can't respond, so much fucking pain. I scream, hunch forward and feel the urge to start pushing. The nurse yells out orders and next thing, I'm being pushed inside.

"Babe, I'm here." Deacon grabs my hand, ooh, big mistake buddy I think as another contraction hits and I squeeze the shit out of his hand.

"Fuck," he mumbles, but he doesn't try to loosen my hold. God love his cotton socks.

"Seriously, babe, you were going to drive yourself here?" Deacon sounds more amazed than pissed.

I nod and squeeze his hand harder.

"Fuck, you're crazy, babe. How the hell did you think you were going to drive in this state?"

I take a few deep breaths and try to be smart. "How crazy? Licking windows crazy or… ah, fuck!"

"Shut up and breathe."

I really wish people would stop telling me to fucking breathe. I grip his hand a bit tighter, digging my nails into him. I hear him hiss and mumble some shit I don't hear.

"You're doing good baby." His voice sounds strained, maybe I'm breaking his hand.

I loosen my grip until I feel my legs lock up and shooting pain travel straight through my body. I now have a strong urge to push.

"I need to push," I pant out as we make it to the birthing suite.

"In a minute, babe, they need to get you on the bed."

"I don't have a fucking minute; this kid is coming NOW!" Yeah, I'm not in a very nice mood.

"Ok babe, we've got this." Deacon helps me to stand.

I rest my hands on the side of the bed, my hips sway as I feel the need to push again. I bear down a little. "I really need to fucking push," I scream as my body locks up with pain, sweat drips from my face. I tear at my shirt.

"It's hot, I feel like I'm on fire. Help me get this shirt off." Deacon lifts the shirt over my head and I feel his warm hand rubbing my back as he takes my shorts and underwear off.

"Okay, babe, we're going to get on the bed so the Doctor can take a look."

"*We?* What's this *we* shit, are you the one that's about to push out this fucking baby?"

"*You*, I meant *you*, babe. This is all you and you're doing so fucking good." He kisses the side of my face as I climb onto the bed. Once there I lay back, yeah, not for long. I hunch forward again and grab my belly when the pain and urge to push hits again.

"Deacon, make it stop please," I beg as he grips my hand. A worried expression crosses his face.

"Deacon, please, I'm begging you. Tell them to get this thing out of me *now*, or you'll arrest them."

The Doctor hurries into the room as the need to push hits again. I don't care what anyone thinks or says, I need to fucking push. I lean forward and feel Deacon slide in behind me. He whispers in my ear "*we got this shit*" and kisses the side of my head.

I nod and when the Doctor tells me to push, I do, with every bit of strength I have.

~*~

I feel like I've been pushing for hours. Deacon talks me through it until finally, with one more big push, I feel the baby slide out. I lean back against Deacon trying to catch my breath, listening to the sweet sound of our baby girl crying. The nurse takes her from the Doctor and hands Deacon a pair of scissors. He leans forward and cuts the cord where the Doctor shows him and then, the nurse places her little naked body on my chest. Tears pour down my face as I look down at her chubby little face. I feel a few wet drops hit my shoulder and when I turn to look at Deacon, tears roll down his cheeks as he looks at our girl. The Doctor delivers the placenta and checks me out.

Then, he says the words that knock the wind from my lungs, "are you ready to go again."

The nurse takes our daughter as another pain shoots through me.

"What the fuck do you mean, am I ready to go again?" I feel like pushing again.

"Doctor, what the fuck is happening?" I hear the worry in Deacon's voice.

"For baby number two." He speaks calmly and I stare at him, wondering what the fuck he is on about.

"Baby, fucking, number fucking, what?" I yell.

"Baby, fucking, what?" Deacon's shocked voice echoes from behind me and I'm glad we're on the same wavelength right now.

"Push, Mrs. Black," he says to me before speaking to Deacon. "It's says right here in the file from the last ultra sound, you're expecting twins."

I feel Deacon freeze up in shock behind me. I squeeze his legs as I push again and it seems to snap him out of it. He kisses my head and whispers in my ear again, "we've got this babe, and any more babies you want to keep pushing out."

"Not fucking happening!" I grit out as I push again and feel baby two slide out. I flop back against Deacon, absolutely exhausted and completely mind fucked right now.

"Congratulations mum and dad, you have a son." The Doctor hands the crying baby to the nurse and Deacon the funny looking scissors again.

After the nurse checks over both babies, she brings them back to me. One is wearing a pink hat, one a blue hat. She places them onto my chest and the tears flow again.

"Two babies, Deacon. We made two babies!" I don't want to take my eyes off them.

"They're gorgeous, sweetheart. Thank you." He kisses the side of my head and when I turn to plant a kiss on his lips, I see the tears in his eyes.

"I love you," I whisper

"Mrs. Black, I love you more than anything in this world," he breathes into my mouth before kissing me again. Then, he turns and speaks to the Doctor, "we'll talk about this later."

The Doctor swallows hard and nods.

"Are you upset about having two?" I wonder if he is as freaked as me right now.

"Baby, I couldn't be a happier man. I have a sexy as fuck wife and two beautiful babies, what more could I ask for?"

Yeah, I melted at his words. Oh, did I forget to mention we got married? The minute the boys were released from the hospital, Deacon proposed. About a month later we married at Civic park at the top of the fountain.

"Mrs. Black?" I look up at the Doctor. "You need to push for me so, the nurse will take the babies and get them wrapped up for you.

"No. Oh, God. Three? No, leave it in there." My eyes widen and the doctor must see the horror on my face. Deacon tenses behind me again.

"No... no," the doctor hurries to clarify. "You need to push the second placenta out now."

"Thank fucking God," I breathe out, making everyone chuckle. "Don't get me wrong, I'm surprised I had two, but I love my babies. But, three? My poor friggen body, you need to give a girl a break." I push and feel the placenta birthing. Deacon and the Doctor are laughing. I'm so fucking glad I'm bloody amusing somebody right now.

~*~

4 months later...

Deacon

After everything that has happened in the past year, I couldn't be more thankful for the life I have now. Since Leia and the twins - Emma and James - came home, life is hectic and crazy. With feeds, nappy changes and naptimes, we never stop, but I wouldn't change a thing.

My wife is the best mom in the world, she bounces between both babies like she's *Superwoman*. Some days I wonder how she does it, love radiates from her and I love her with everything I am. One lifetime with my soul mate will never be enough.

I walk downstairs and hear *All Shook Up* by *Elvis* playing. When I reach the living room, I rest my shoulder against the door frame and watch both my babies in their bouncers smiling and blowing spit bubbles as they watch my wife sing and dance in front of them. I place a hand to my chest as my heart skips a beat, knowing everything in this house is my world. I would fall to my knees time and time again, for the woman who gave me everything I never knew I wanted, or needed.